LOVE WRIT LARGE

THE
SEAGULL
LIBRARY OF
GERMAN
LITERATURE

NAVID KERMANI

LOVE WRIT LARGE

Translated by Alexander Booth

LONDON NEW YORK CALCUTTA

This publication has been supported by a grant from
the Goethe-Institut India

Seagull Books, 2022

First published in German as *Große Liebe* by Navid Kermani
© Carl Hanser Verlag, Munich, 2014

First published in English translation by Seagull Books, 2019
English translation © Alexander Booth, 2019

Published as part of the Seagull Library of German Literature, 2022

ISBN 978 1 8030 9 006 1

Typeset by Seagull Books, Calcutta, India
Printed and bound by WordsWorth India, New Delhi, India

Contents

I

Once upon a time a king was travelling throughout his lands with his retinue of ministers, generals, soldiers, clerks, servants and the women of his harem. At some point he saw an old, ragged, and quite possibly mad, man crouching by the side of the road. 'And? What do you have to say for yourself? I bet you want to be me,' the king called down mockingly from his elephant. 'No,' the old man replied, 'I no longer want to be myself.'

2

The first time he fell in love he was fifteen, and never again so hard. She was the most beautiful girl in the whole schoolyard, standing off in the smoking area, often just two or three steps away, never giving him a single thought. The younger students were forbidden from approaching the smokers, let alone lighting a cigarette, so he tried to be as unassuming as possible, there in between the broad shoulders, still as a stowaway. He'd only raise his head after having a quick look around for any teachers then steal a surreptitious glance at her, always seemingly at the centre of her little clique. As little hope as he entertained of ever winning her favour, the thought that she might look more than just kindly upon one of the *Abiturienten* preparing for their graduation exams drove him crazy. To calm down he told himself that her infectious cheerfulness and choice words were instead handed out for the one here and for the other there. Nevertheless, the boy always kept his eyes on them to make sure they weren't secretly touching her hands, her back or, God forbid, her bum. At the same time, he constantly expected someone to turn around to ask him what he was doing there. The teachers had already driven him off on a number of occasions simply with their angry or surprised looks. He wanted to spare himself the embarrassment of being pulled out of the crowd in front of the most beautiful girl in the whole schoolyard and sent back to the kids his own age. His situation was already awkward enough, convinced as he was that the smokers were staring at him non-stop. In reality, however—and here the logic ended—they had their backs to him the entire time.

3

Why have I been thinking about the fifteen-year-old since the day before yesterday? Or, rather, why did I write about him yesterday? I've thought about him a lot, maybe even every day, since that time thirty years ago when I was the boy who'd spend his breaks in the smoking area though he neither smoked nor knew any of the older students; despondent, full of longing and with a heart beating so loudly that some days he'd lay his right hand across his chest in fear. The day before yesterday, while reading the Persian poet Attar's anecdote about the old man not wanting to be himself, I was overcome by the thought that my first and never-to-be-greater love had been grounded in the desire to escape myself. In fact, later—once you think you've found yourself—you want, or I did in any event, to hold on to yourself. I was positively adamant about myself and all the more so when it had to do with love. The reader will object, saying that a clueless boy is not to be compared to a holy fool, that his desire to escape himself as a pubescent—ignoring the fact that one usually describes puberty, on the contrary, as a search for the self—was fundamentally different from the path of the mystic. Indeed, something outright banal. Though that may be, yesterday I began writing with the hope that I might convince the reader otherwise.

4

The reader should not imagine the boy to have been at all self-conscious, confused or cowardly. In his own class he was on the confident side, some of his peers thought he was arrogant, some of his teachers recalcitrant, and he often disregarded whatever his parents had to say. And he wasn't completely inexperienced either; with his long, dark curls he definitely attracted not just a few stares. In fact, he'd already 'gone out', as they still used to say, with girls his own age many times. That he hadn't slept with any of them wasn't uncommon for that point in one's life, and hardly caused him to think twice. For as much as the secret of the union of two bodies occupied his thoughts, he simultaneously sensed its meaning in life and had decided he'd wait for a connection worthy of the name of love. He wasn't thinking about the most beautiful girl in the whole schoolyard. By the time he'd already begun spending his breaks in the smoking area, he never once imagined—in his dreams or, to be more precise, under his sheets—kissing her, much less seeing her standing naked in front of him. He had enough of a sense of reality to realize that the most beautiful one wouldn't be interested in anyone who was still too young to stand with the smokers. The reader may expect a plausible explanation as to why the boy nevertheless mixed in with all the others, between their wide shoulders, there where he really must have felt as self-conscious, confused and cowardly as I described it on yesterday's page. For four days now I've been trying to explain the course of events, but my memory is like a film where censors have cut out all the important scenes. The one in which the young boy is walking through the long hallway that connected the two sides of the *Gymnasium* towards the most beautiful girl in the whole schoolyard is right in front of me, the way their eyes met and then immediately turned away, but then met a second, and a third time; I never forget the smile he thought he saw on her lips before she stepped out of his field of vision; I vaguely remember the sweet fantasies to which he abandoned himself while crossing the last metres of the hallway and then in class, though he didn't believe for longer than a few seconds that he'd ever really be her boyfriend, that they'd walk hand in hand, that he'd see the surprised looks of his classmates. Then, in that film the censors have cut, he's already standing back between the broad shoulders. I can only speculate how much effort it cost him to walk over to the smoking area and what's more: so long as one of the stricter teachers wasn't keeping watch, to go back every break, to withstand the looks cast at him every break, to defy the whispered derision he thought he could hear, just two or three steps away from the most beautiful one, under the dark shadow of her hair—well, actually she was a blonde —her little face a lamp or maybe a torch surrounded by raven's wings, as the poet Nizami wrote about the legendary Layla in the twelfth century: 'Whose heart would not have filled with longing at the sight of this girl? But young Majnun felt even more. He was drowned in the ocean of love before he knew that there was such a thing. He had already given his heart to Layla before he understood what he was giving away.'

5

One day Majnun walked by Layla's home. As he was looking up at the sky, someone said to him: 'Majnun, what are you doing looking up at the sky? There's the wall to Layla's house!' He answered: 'I am content with the light of a star which falls upon it.'

6

Before I continue with the story about the young boy's love, I must return for a moment to the hallway that connected the two buildings of the *Gymnasium*. It's become clear to me that he cannot just have imagined the most beautiful one's smile, as he'd already discovered the tiny space between her two front teeth the first time their eyes met—thirty years later the logic comes seamlessly—as a result of her opening her mouth as he passed. How could I forget! Later, the space between her teeth would often be an issue for, whenever she spoke, she seemed to be trying to keep her lips from moving more than necessary and was especially embarrassed by laughing. Whenever he noticed her shame, he would wordily praise the perfection of that single flaw, which in truth was no flaw at all but the birthmark of the lovers in Persian poetry. At the same time he would tease her in a loving tone of voice and try to get her to laugh by mimicking her nearly closed lips or telling jokes he had learnt just for her, softly by her side in bed, or tickling the bottom of her foot with his toes. By the time her gleaming teeth finally appeared, a hand, forearm or, at the most, an arm's length away from his eyes, he'd beam with happiness, every single time, so childishly excited and almost triumphant that she would have laughed by then at the latest anyway. And when he kissed her, my God, I think I can still feel the vault the gap between her teeth made with her tongue. He loved that, more than any other feeling he loved the moment his tongue would move across her teeth and suddenly, almost unexpectedly, delve into the crack; that moment, the one in which his soft, supple tongue could feel the hard, smooth enamel on both sides, even if only a few millimetres deep. And it's here he'd sink as if into an ocean, and that is precisely what Nizami meant. But I've already gone far too far with talk about their love.

7

Now that I think about it, the fifteen-year-old who was me couldn't have spent more than a few silent days or a week at most in the smoking area during his breaks. It was excitement that made every minute feel longer; it's memory that expands time. The most beautiful one never gave any sign of remembering their having met in the hallway that connected the two buildings of the *Gymnasium*, never gave him any look that would have allowed him to talk with her. He never got any chance to see that gap which perfected her beauty. Now that I think about it, she had to have recognized the boy who, from one day to the next, was standing there among the smokers though he neither smoked nor ever talked to anyone, which likely meant he wasn't supposed to be mixing with the older students at all. They probably just asked themselves who the boy was; she for her part would have already sensed that he'd shown up for her. The boy himself naively believed she'd neither observed nor even seen him and was subsequently disappointed that he was the only one who remembered their having met. And that was why he couldn't have seriously hoped that their acquaintanceship, to say nothing of a connection, was worthy of the name of love. What drove him to mix in among the broad shoulders during every break was only the urge to observe her from the corners of his eyes; at best, the prospect of stealing an additional glance, another smile. It would be presumptuous to speak of love at that point, even if in Persian poetry love necessarily begins the first time the two lovers meet. Now that I think about it, at the beginning, it was little more than a thrill. A test of his courage. The lust for adventure. Later, once she'd already left him, she accused him of never having really loved her, thereby adding a sense of indignation to his despair.

8

This, then, is the question that's been bothering me, or should bother me, more than any proof of a deeper, mystical meaning. Can what the fifteen-year-old feels, as wonderfully and terribly as it shall explode across the pages to come, even be called love, indeed, the love of his life, something I was convinced of until the day before yesterday? Now, in fact, I must mention the letter he placed in a box thirty years ago and has never opened since. It's still lying there, it's just that the box was replaced by a moving crate which was recently replaced by a wooden chest, but it's still there underneath all the other letters he has received over the years (both times I made sure not to dump the envelopes but to pick them up from below with both hands so that they would more or less remain in chronological order). As far as I can recall—perhaps my memory is dramatizing it all again—the letter is an angry settling of accounts. She placed responsibility for the breakdown of their love (though, in his case, it hadn't been love) on him alone; he had crushed the flower, proven himself unworthy of the treasure, he still had so much to learn about life—that's more or less what her letter must have sounded like and where today I'd likely discover the traces of her favourite writers. But back then he didn't understand a single word. She'd been the one to dismiss him and go back to the older students in the smoking area so that he wouldn't dare speak to her first, something she denied on the phone. From one day to the next, she was the one who'd turned cold. Merciless. Pitiless. She'd turned him out like a dog that's grown tiresome, that's what it felt like, then thrown stones at him so he'd leave her street (he had his favourite writers too). And once he was gone—if only because he was ill and ended up skipping school for weeks—her letter arrived, most likely a response to pleading missives I no longer remember, to declare him at fault. I could go and get it, the chest's out in the hall only three, at most four steps away from my desk. I can still see the envelope, it's yellowish or adorned with yellow, I'm not sure, and there's a female's handwriting in brown felt-tip pen on it, which at the time struck the boy as extremely grown up. But maybe it's best I wait until I'm done telling the story of the love of my life before confronting any settling of accounts.

9

'I myself sense the extraordinary subtleness one finds in love,' the Andalusian Ibn 'Arabi—still revered as the greatest master, *ash-Shaykh al-Akbar*—confessed in the thirteenth century. 'One feels a great yearning, a piercing passion, love as an overwhelming power, a total wasting away, and one is prevented from enjoying either sleep or food. One knows neither who it is nor the means by which one loves. Your beloved does not appear to you in a clear way. This is the most exquisite grace, which I experience as both a taste on the tongue and an immediate sensory impression.'

10

The *Gymnasium* was on the side of a little river that ran through the town but which hardly anyone noticed—and which a little further on you couldn't see at all as the main road had been built across it —and the smoking area wasn't anything official, just the space in front of and behind an opening in the wall which led to the riverbank. In his later distress, the boy would often sit there, nothing idyllic to speak of, just a little stretch of unpaved dirt between the warehouse of a shipping company and the car park of a home improvement store; at that point, however, when he first began to silently spend his breaks in the smoking area, he had no idea that the river was hidden behind the school at all. From his spot in between those broad shoulders he only saw the trees and the bushes behind the brick wall, now and again one of the older students disappearing into the shrubbery or coming back. Once, when the most beautiful girl in the whole schoolyard didn't appear, he took the opportunity to ask where the opening went. Today I could give him a clue where to find her; in truth, for one whole minute he'd forgotten her completely, then he stepped through the opening, watched the other, more sparsely formed huddles of students smoking, followed a little path that ran through the trees and shrubs, and after twenty or thirty steps reached the thin strip of riverbank, which here and there was sparsely covered in grass. And that's where he discovered her, a few metres down-river, almost at the fence of the shipping company. That's where he saw her halfway from behind, halfway from the side, on her blonde hair the sun, which at that time of year was still cold, but which in the boy's mind at least conferred her with something like a halo, sitting on a rock, her small nose bent slightly upward at the tip like a ski jump, wearing her at-the-time fashionable purple corduroy trousers, a light jacket across her knees, beneath the tight pullover her breasts two hills with little towers at their peaks, between her thin fingers a cigarette she'd bring to her mouth as if lost in thought. To her mouth! I imagine that was the moment, the glance, which brought the vision home, the most beautiful girl in the whole schoolyard illuminated on the rock, before her the little prosaic river with the four-lane road on the other side, behind her a bonfire site littered with empty beer cans and plastic sausage packets, as a backdrop the parked lorries of the shipping company —I imagine it was here that that quiet longing, in no way directed towards fulfilment, turned into that desire he'd never before experienced but which was well-described in all his books. Her mouth! If it would only open for him once more, just once, at first in a smile but then for a kiss, yes, at least for a kiss. And so the plan: to coax a kiss out of her, just one. He was too agitated, too obsessed with his so-to-speak casual goal to think any further, much less think about that connection worthy of the name of love. Then his sense of reason dawned on him that it would be better not to talk to her there, as he would only end up quivering and stammering. She hadn't even noticed him yet.

II

He hadn't yet taken the whole twenty, thirty steps back to the smoking area when the uselessness and, even worse for a fifteen-year-old, absurdity of his plan began to dawn on him: of all things, stealing a kiss from the most beautiful girl in the whole schoolyard, a girl who could drive already, who was about to complete her graduation exams, and afterwards would probably move to a bigger town to study or go into the great beyond of the working world. He hadn't even got her to say her name and here he was imagining himself victorious. Back in between the broad shoulders he felt more self-conscious than usual, more confused, more afraid. And if she really did have a boyfriend? Of course she had a boyfriend outside of school—an older guy who went to work or was studying, that's why she could share her obviously infectious cheerfulness and choice words with her classmates. Clearly she'd already had a lot of boyfriends. As excited as he'd been not even three minutes ago, painting the whole scene to himself —touching her mouth, her breasts, her entire body from head to toe—he was now distinctly tortured by the thought that someone else had been allowed something he had no prospect of ever encountering. Until now, it had only been a game, a whim, an adventure. *He* was no more than a child pressing his head against the window of an expensive shop, he thought to himself with contempt. Lowering his glance, once again he felt the eyes of the older students upon him. Just look at their shoes! They all wore shiny black shoes with pointed tips, just like in the music videos of the time, while others wore bright suede boots, clogs or, despite the cool temperature, sandals with orthopedically balanced soles. For his part, he was still happy with the trainers his mother bought him. Thirty years later, you might smile at the fifteen-year-old's plight the same way you do as when coming across an odd fashion trend only a family photo album could remind you of. Returning from the little river where he first got to stare at the most beautiful girl in the whole schoolyard for a long time, in his shoes he thought he could recognize, I don't want to say the proof, but indeed a symbol, a visible sign of that part of humanity to which he did not belong. This time he trotted back to his classroom well before the bell rang.

12

As Layla's parents refused to allow Majnun to come near her tent, he borrowed a sheepskin from a shepherd and asked him if he could mix in with the herd. When they came past Layla's tent, Majnun caught a glimpse of her and fell unconscious. The shepherd brought him away and threw water into his face in an attempt to cool his burning love. From that day on, Majnun wandered the desert clad in the fleece alone. Someone asked him why he wore no clothes. 'It is thanks to the sheepskin that I was able to cast a glance on Layla,' Majnun answered. 'No garment on earth could ever be more precious.'

13

The boy left it all behind him after his double hour of maths class, which came after the first of the two long breaks. Looking out the window from his seat in the back row, he'd heard the lesson but in the way you listen to people chatting in a foreign language or traffic noise. The teacher had called on him once, had obviously asked him a question, but the boy only responded with a horrified look, mouth wide, lips frozen. The teacher had made some sort of joke, one or two other students laughed. In the small break between the two lessons, the boy told his classmate that he was indeed fine. The image of the most beautiful one sitting down by the water had been before his eyes, behind her the lorries, on the other side of the river the four-lane road: expansion. Then he'd seen himself in his completely childlike, now strangely conscious, blinding bashfulness, his confusion, his cowardice among all the broad shoulders:

constriction. *Qabḍ wa-basṭ*, 'constriction and expansion' is what the Sufis call the two basic states in whose dialectic mystical experience, when not to say all experience, takes place; for Hegel, history too. In *qabḍ wa-basṭ* Ibn 'Arabi specifically recognized a presentiment the soul has of things before they come to the outer senses. With that, constriction and expansion are also the precursors of all love before it actually occurs. And Ibn 'Arabi went even further, describing the intensity, determination and disorientation of youthful infatuation—that kind alone!—as comparable, as related to the mystic's 'drowning' (*istighrāq*) in the overflowing love of the divine and not only in terms of the symptoms. When the bell rang the boy jumped up and, before the teacher had even finished speaking, marched out of the room. Like a relapsing addict he felt certain that if he just returned to his place among the broad shoulders, if he just spent his breaks in the smoking area as long as necessary, his desire would be reciprocated. At the same time, mind you, he was absent of any hope whatsoever. He was about to commit an act, his reason told him, which would remain utterly pointless. From a religious point of view, one could add that he was about to become a fool.

14

It belongs to the myth my memory has wrapped around my great love that the most beautiful girl in the whole schoolyard spoke to the boy precisely that break following the two hours of maths class. Naturally, however, there are explanations I have never cared to consider: that he came into the smoking area where she was standing with a cigarette poised between her two thin fingers earlier than usual; that, as no little group had formed yet, there were no shoulders to divide the two of them; that she would've had to have been looking away for their eyes not to meet. Considering that they'd already met each other in the hallway connecting the two buildings of the *Gymnasium*, had even smiled at each other, they, I don't want to say inevitably, but indeed naturally, came into conversation, particularly as the most beautiful one—as she later said to justify herself as it were—hadn't thought he was too young to be in the smoking area at all. As to the possible reasons why she spoke to him, one could recall the previous break she'd spent alone on the river and from there speculate a need for communication or distraction. One could just as well add her infectious cheerfulness, which she only addressed to him as he was standing there staring at her so pathetically. My memory registers these external circumstances without giving them any meaning. It is happier to explain her speaking to him as a miracle his love created. That the first words they exchanged were completely normal or even completely insignificant increases their secretive nature. 'We saw each other recently,' she said. 'Of course we've seen each other,' he answered in a surprisingly firm voice and in the same breath began to speak about the weather, of all things the weather, just to keep her from asking him what class he was in or offering him a cigarette. At the same time as he was making his observation about the spring which, like every year, was a long time in coming, he was angry at himself for not thinking of anything more original. 'Yeah, I'm already looking forward to the warm weather,' she said, seemingly happy to talk about it, 'to the colours, the first ice cream.' He told her about the weather forecast, which nevertheless seemed favourable. 'Good to know,' she said as the first older students began to roll in. 'And who would have thought that such overwhelming sweetness could flow from so small a mouth?' as the poet Nizami wrote about the legendary Layla. 'Is it possible, then, to break whole armies with one small grain of sugar?'

15

The next day he was the first person to walk into the smoking area during both breaks, and the day after that and the day after that one (I realize now that he must have spent more than a week among the broad shoulders there, and maybe another one on top of the first). That the most beautiful girl in the whole schoolyard no longer came that early—that she didn't offer him any other chance to talk, maybe even came late on purpose or, what was an even more upsetting possibility, felt absolutely no attraction for him one way or the other and simply didn't pay attention to him, maybe did not even notice him at all—hit him harder than any angry look, discouraging gesture, or word with which she could once and for all have said: No point in getting your hopes up! For since the second time they'd met, he was ready for anything, had run through all the various forms their acquaintance could take on that might merit the name of love. He'd only forgotten to calculate one thing: her complete indifference. God only knows how many sentences he formulated to have an excuse to go up to her only to discard them all once more. He could no longer control his eyes, which constantly went to her instead of the ground or even the teachers. In any event, thirty years later, it seems to me as if he'd had Majnun in mind who, when asked which way to pray, responded: 'If you are an ignorant lump of earth: the Kaaba. If you are a lover: God. If, however, you happen to be Majnun: You align yourself in prayer towards Layla'—as if the boy in the schoolyard had stared unceasingly at the most beautiful one. When I imagine the situation, his glance really couldn't have been that penetrating, otherwise she or some of the other students no doubt would have asked him to talk or laughed at him or simply sought another space behind the wall where the other smokers were. On the other hand, his perception of the situation couldn't have functioned perfectly as, after having overlooked one of the stricter teachers, he was indeed exposed to the embarrassment of being pulled out of the crowd in front of the most beautiful one. But did she even notice his having been downgraded at all? Everything happened so quickly, in my memory in just a matter of seconds, the teacher shouting at him, surprising him with the question as to what he was doing in the smoking area, the fifteen-year-old's presence of mind, which at the very least returned to him that moment, his mumbled apology and the way he walked away, without looking up, the bottomless grief into which he willingly collapsed around the corner of the next building. No, she probably hadn't noticed a thing, I can see that, but sadly only thirty years after the fact. Back then, he suffered from her not noticing him and could have concluded that she hadn't given a single thought to his quiet exchange of words with the teacher, which couldn't have lasted more than four sentences, at most a minute, either. But, as we've said, lovers aren't always that well versed in logic.

16

Assuming I never had a photograph of myself as a fifteen-year-old and by chance was given one to see, I probably wouldn't recognize myself. I imagine a lot still connects me to the kid I once was: how he acts in a group, what he's like when he watches a football match, how he is in friendship etc., even the look and the posture in class and team photos, his way of thinking and his opinions about the world are to a large degree in my ear still. But it's more than that. In spite of all adjustments, they've remained my own. Later, as I gradually grew up or, to stick to the closest example, let's say since the time school regulations allowed me to smoke, I became the person I believe myself to be now. I can see the high-school student in front of me and do not hesitate to say: me, the grammar-school and then university student, husband and divorcee, son and, often over the last few weeks, father, and wouldn't have any idea what else to say but: me. And yet the boy who at the start of every break runs to the smoking area so as not to waste a single moment with the most beautiful one, that ignorant, passionate, eccentric, thanks-to-a-single-glance enraptured and just a little while later desperate, even world-weary and because of his absurd behaviour (more the result of his reading than any strategy of conquest) indeed truly foolish, enamoured boy—who is that supposed to be? That I'd never acted like he did before can be explained by age. But since then I've never resembled him again either. I've been in love, surely more profoundly, in any event, over a much longer period of time, I have also fought more passionately, have lost more than he did and, at least physically speaking, have experienced more all-encompassing ecstasy. By all means, I was not always the emotionally impassive one I consider myself to be today. Nevertheless, I do not recognize myself in the boy, he is not I and the distancing use of the third person is more than a literary trick. There's a reason why Ibn 'Arabi expressly described youthful infatuation as comparable, as related to the mystic's 'drowning' and not only as far as the symptoms are concerned. Maybe we are really ourselves when we believe it least.

17

Of the four primary aspects of love which Ibn
'Arabi mentions (there is a considerable number of
secondary names for love that Arabic gave the
Andalusian), only the 'sudden passion of love' or
'unexpected inclination to love' could be attributed
to the boy (that is, if any of them could really be
attributed to the boy), what Ibn 'Arabi calls *hawā* and
which, to be more precise, is only the first of many
meanings he applied to the term. This first meaning
of one of the four primary aspects of love leads to the
phrase 'which overwhelms the heart or suddenly
appears within and arises from the as-of-yet unman-
ifest reality of the beloved and penetrates to the heart
of the lover alone through its outer appearance'. In
other words, it is the same passion that precedes
union with the beloved, the beginning of infatuation,
and usually has one of three causes, namely, the
glance (*naẓar*), the ear (*samāʿ*) or a favour. Or more
generally speaking: the proper way of behaving

(*iḥsān*). And Ibn ʿArabi is enough of a realist to know that in most cases the glance is the catalyst while that passion which is aroused through the ear—even in his extremely sensitive aural culture—occurs rather seldom and, as a rule, progresses rather poorly; in only the rarest of cases does a face correspond to the charm its voice may promise. That love which develops thanks to favour—which is to say, the proper way of behaving or, even more generally, the characteristic virtues of the beloved—is, however, the weakest. Ibn ʿArabi points out that *hawā* is derived from the root h-w-y, which literally means 'disappearing' or 'to fall from above', as a verb something like in Surah 53:1: 'By the star when it descends.' *Hawā* as a noun already has the lexical meaning of a 'suffering from love' (though love hasn't even properly begun yet!). The noun *huwīy*—'to fall into'—also stems from the same root, he adds.

18

He learnt her name—I wish I could recount some adventure like stealing her notebook, say, or a risky shadowing or something in that vein—by asking the German teacher who also taught the *Abiturienten*. During the short break the boy simply explained that she'd given him a lift home and, as it was already dark, had dropped him off in front of his house; he wanted to leave her a little note and some chocolate in thanks. The girl he was talking about was as tall as he was, had semi-long blonde hair, brown eyes and a slightly upturned nose, she often wore purple trousers and had a tiny, almost invisible gap between her two front teeth. 'But promise her you won't try to hitch any more rides in the dark,' the teacher said after immediately identifying the most beautiful girl in the whole schoolyard as one of his own. Now the boy was sitting through his second hour of German class in possession of her name, which slightly disappointed him, and didn't know what good it would do; he couldn't really write her a note seeing that he had nothing to share other than the fact that he was in love with her—but with what realistic expectations? That he wanted to see her again—but for what rational reason? That she was beautiful—but with what plausible pretense? And at the same time, he was scared the German teacher would talk to her the next time he saw her for the advanced course, that he would tell her about the note, that he would praise her exemplary care. A thousand abominable thoughts flew through the boy's mind as he sat through his German lesson; he envisioned a thousand different situations, each one more embarrassing than the next. He had to do something, that much was clear. If he couldn't write a note, then he still somehow had to make use of her name in order to prove its discovery worthwhile. But the thing that was more pressing, a lot more pressing, was the fact that he had to come up with an excuse as soon as possible so that she wouldn't resent his trick. It is worth mentioning that Ibn 'Arabi in no uncertain terms traced the confusion that arrests the lover's spirit and that necessary as well as continual state of insecurity associated with contemplating the most appropriate means for getting close to the beloved. Under that sign of confusion Ibn 'Arabi listed the assumption that the beloved appeared to everyone else as equally ideal and that, in them, they too found those very qualities the lover did.

19

A thief once had his hand hacked off as punishment. Holding it up in his other hand when he left he was asked why he continued to carry it around. He replied: 'Upon it I have tattooed the name of my beloved.'

20

Of all the absurd things, it was the great revolutions of those years which, after all, had been inspired by the revolution in the land of his favourite writers, that ended up keeping the young boy out of trouble. In West Germany it was the time of mass protests against nuclear armament. Hundreds of thousands of mostly young people had demonstrated numerous times against what was known as the NATO Double-Track Decision in the now former capital's Hofgarten. Having been politicized rather early on by events taking place in the land of his favourite writers, the boy had joined one of the peace movements, which were also quite widespread even in smaller towns. As demonstrators had thus far been unsuccessful in getting the government to give in, the next step was to block the entrance to the Federal Ministry of Defence. I can't remember why, maybe there was a NATO summit, maybe an important resolution in the parliament, maybe more ministries had been considered or all of them were supposed to be blocked at the same time. In any event, I only know that her town's Citizens for Peace alliance had been assigned to the Ministry of Defence, but God knows better, as Ibn 'Arabi would've added. The evening of the same day—yet another coincidence that the boy denied so as to be able to consider his love an act of divine providence—he learnt the most beautiful one's name, the blockaders of all the various peace groups were going to be meeting up at the Protestant Students' Union in order to discuss the trip into the capital and go over the codes of conduct. Considering Majnun and other various lovers, one might think that the boy in his state wasn't aware of the great revolutions of the time any more and just threw himself howling and wailing into a corner instead, that is, whenever he wasn't already standing in a corner of the smoking area to begin with; but that's not how it was, it never is, or, if it was, then at most for just a few hours. His participation in the class following his two hours of German was passable and the thought of not blocking the Ministry of Defence on account of his love pangs simply did not occur to him. His love pangs were probably not so great, or not yet anyway, and memory is to blame for projecting all that misery onto the beginning of their story later on so that, like Majnun and other famous literary lovers, it too might unfold in the exact same way as all those love stories did. But God tells the better stories as well, as Ibn 'Arabi at this point would have remarked, and that night the boy went to the meeting of all the various peace groups where he ran into—well, the reader already knows whom—in the lobby. 'Hello, Jutta,' he said thoughtlessly. 'Hello,' she replied, curious to learn how he knew her name.

21

Today I can no longer find the cockiness, when not to say guts, that was so characteristic of the boy, not only in our story here but in many situations that didn't have anything to do with love at all. And I don't mean nerve in general—that, for example, at just fifteen he was preparing to take part in an illegal blockade at the Federal Ministry of Defence without even telling his parents. In terms of putting one's own well-being in danger, most readers would probably have risked much more. I mean a kind of chutzpah, the ability to say or do exactly what his heart whispered without a second thought just at the crucial moment for a matter or relationship to develop further and, when necessary, to be ready for disarming honesty or a bold-faced lie, for vigorous exaggeration or unreserved directness—and to get away with it! I mean that kind of acceleration switch he had while dealing with other people, a supercharger of sorts (to say something without turning to Ibn 'Arabi for once), and, on top of it, I mean that, together with other aspects I might be overlooking or cannot explain to myself, precisely here, his deviation from any kind of plan didn't come from a feeling of superiority like it does in the routine heartbreaker but, being fifteen, from the greatest possible inexperience and insecurity—I mean that, once again, it was precisely thanks to his artistic naivety that he was able to charm the most beautiful girl in the whole schoolyard into becoming interested in him, of all people. In the end, she—who could drive and would soon be taking her graduation exam—would not experience such a sense of impetuousness with any of her classmates or even the older boys who were already at university or inhabiting the beyond of the working world. She likely did not possess such impetuousness any more herself, but at most simply remembered it. 'I asked your German teacher,' the boy explained. 'Why?' she asked, but her smile suggested she already knew. 'Because in the whole schoolyard there is no one more beautiful than you,' he said, causing her to reveal the gap between her teeth.

22

These days I can only shake my head when by turns I see the scene in the lobby of the Protestant Students' Union and then my own son, about to turn fifteen himself, in front of me. It's not just age. In line with the fashion of the time—which by that point the boy had been following even more devotedly for a few days—on top of his blue-and-white striped dungarees he wore three cotton sweaters chequered green, purple and ochre with, as if by decree, the longest at the bottom and the shortest on top; his curls were as big as Jimi Hendrix's and his small-as-a-button, metal-rimmed specs took their cue from John Lennon; but though he gave it a brush every morning, his scraggly beard had nothing in common with Karl Marx's. The most important component, however, remained his brand-new Birkenstocks, those wide, flat sandals with their orthopedically balanced footbed that had cost him two months' allowance. Once upon a time, people had dressed scarecrows that way; looking back now, I can comprehend my parents' anguish, though this doesn't make my own son's fashion sense any more understandable to me (good God, the underwear peeking out of his necessarily baggy pants). And it's this scarecrow of a lover, this inexperienced, as far as the world and Eros were concerned clueless, clownish autodidact of a Casanova and sprig of a man who actually snags a girl, almost a woman, in the lobby of the Protestant Students' Union, a girl—I swear!—who'd have been the most beautiful girl in every schoolyard in the world.

23

'Beauty's eye does not see beauty, for it can only observe the perfection of its own beauty in love's mirror of a lover,' the Persian Ahmad Ghazali, younger brother of the famous Mohammad Ghazali, taught in the twelfth century. 'Thus, beauty clearly requires the lover so that the beloved can feed on his or her own beauty in the mirror of that wistful love.' At this point, one could refer to the word of God, which, however, Ahmad Ghazali in his concentrated thoughts does not do, assuming that it's obvious: 'I was a hidden treasure and loved to be known. Hence I created the world.' To Ahmad Ghazali, lovers and beloveds are more strictly, strongly and even cruelly separated than they are to other mystics and nature makes a distinction between their love in a similar way. The love of the lover truly exists, while the love of the beloved is only the reflection of that ardent passion mirrored within them. Just as the lover and beloved are unequal as unalike and remain separate even to the point of enmity and mutual harm, love requires 'helplessness and need, doubt, humiliation and utter submission' on the part of the lover. The part of the beloved, on the contrary, brings with itself 'tyranny, grandeur and arrogance', they experience union as the overwhelming event which shatters their horizon, their power of imagination, their self-image, yes, even their very selves. And then Ahmad Ghazali adds to the bargain the fact that he himself does not know 'who the lover or the beloved is, for here one begins and the other ends, or this one begins . . . and therein lies a great secret.'

24

Naturally, nothing had yet been won, much less an acquaintanceship begun, as the young boy strode into the meeting room of the Protestant Students' Union alongside the most beautiful one. As to the question of which class he was in, nothing other than the truth occurred to him, it's just that afterwards he continued the conversation without mentioning the German teacher they had in common so that she couldn't ask about his status in the smoking area either. Nevertheless, she didn't talk to him like a child and seemed to take it for granted that they'd look for two adjoining seats. So she hadn't agreed to meet anyone else, he told himself to gain courage. Then, during the meeting, he succeeded in making a comment that in turn was taken seriously by all the blockaders and discussed for a number of minutes or even longer, a passionate plea for non-violence and why, even if provoked, it would need to be adhered to—and yes, he could feel, thought he could even see in the corner of his eye, that she looked at him in agreement, maybe even appreciation. In fact, she smiled at him once he thought he'd waited long enough and finally turned his head to look at her. Every human being accomplishes feats in their lives that no one else acknowledges, that others do not even see, that from outside are not worthy of attention and have absolutely no influence on the world whatsoever; in a way, they are acts between humankind and God. The speech—yes, it truly was a little speech, complete with formulations like 'don't do the pigs the favour' and 'violence is now truly counter-productive when solidarity with the peace movement is growing wonderfully within the existing power structure'—the speech the young boy gave at the meeting of all those various peace groups was one of those acts, and as far as he alone is concerned, nothing less than an heroic feat. At most I can explain the courage, if not the rhetorical fire or political acumen, that makes it possible for a fifteen-year-old to stand up before a group of at least forty, fifty, almost without exception grown-up, activists. As often as he would speak in public later, he never once gave another speech in which he, according to his own judgement, so clearly outdid himself. Be that as it may, he also never again had as important a reason to. And so it might have been overexertion that kept him from asking the most beautiful one after the meeting if she wanted to go have a beer with him. That early in their acquaintanceship she would have certainly declined. The prospect, however, of sitting next to her on the ride into the capital seemed real. Nevertheless, she offered to give him a lift home. 'I came with my bike,' he said as casually as possible and was proud the next morning to have controlled himself. And after that evening, he would no longer spend his breaks in the smoking area. The conqueror finally had a strategy.

25

Three quarters of an hour before leaving—it was three-thirty in the morning and raining—his mother, thinking it was a school trip, dropped him off behind their town's multipurpose hall. 'Are you the first one here?' she wondered seeing the car park completely empty. 'Everyone's meeting out front,' the boy explained and maintained that because of the one-way street it was easier for him to just walk around the building than to have her drop him off there (Google Maps confirms my suspicion that there is no one-way street around the multipurpose hall in the town I was born at all). Little by little the other block-aders arrived, the bus came on time, they waited five, fifteen minutes for the others who, as usual, were late. But she wasn't there. She simply was not there. Twenty minutes after the agreed departure time he swore to the leader, organizer, coordinator or what-ever poseur from one of the various peace groups he was, a fat, bearded man as old as his father, likely a leftover from the penultimate anti-war movement, in one hand an umbrella and in the other his list, almost yelled at this man that they absolutely had to wait for the latecomers—'But there's only a single latecomer,' this poseur added—that Jutta had prepared for the action so well—'But if she's simply not here'—and anyway that kind of bourgeois way of thinking was intolerable—'But we must be at the ministry before they start work, or else the blockade is pointless.' If there had been mobiles at the time, the boy would have sent her an SMS, would have called her, woken her up, been able to send a taxi to her front door—but back then what could he do when it was already almost thirty minutes past the agreed time? 'Well, you can all kiss my ass with your "secondary virtues",' he said, leaving the poseur standing under his umbrella and, soaking wet, climbed into the bus (it was around that time that a member of the power apparatus who sympathized with the peace movement had caused a scandal by declaring that punctuality, discipline and order were secondary virtues with which you could also run a concentration camp).

26

On the twenty-sixth day—that's right, I'm writing all of this one page a day to allow my memory the opportunity to sort itself, and determining how long a page is in accordance with the most famous poets—today, in other words, I find myself looking for a telephone number, mailing address or an e-mail. Not only could her last, not to mention first, name be a bit disappointing, but she could have married and, equal rights notwithstanding, taken the opportunity to no longer be named like everyone else. Now, to go and grab her letter from the chest and look at its return address would be pointless as she'd been living in a squat, which can no longer exist due to the undeniable fact that, together with the whole city block, it gave way to the expressway they'd been protesting. My goodness, those demonstrations against the expressway—what a complete failure and yet what a feast for my memory! After the day of her graduation exam, that is, the day of the senior prank when he saw her drive by on the open bed of a lorry, she never met him again; his calls, his letters, his visits—which, sadly, I have not repressed —a whole afternoon long on the sidewalk below her window: all useless. When some time later she showered him with the aforementioned accusations, he wrote back but didn't dare to call and, in the end, avoided a second letter. He still kept an eye out for her in the bars though he'd already learnt from her flatmate that she'd moved to the city and, no, she couldn't give him her number. Didn't they have any common friends whom I could track down? In any event, I still know the name of the village she came from, it's just a few hills behind our town. 'Perhaps her parents still live there,' I hope and quickly glance through an online telephone book. Look! Connected to the village there's one, no, three listings with the surname, all the first names are male and were already rare in my generation, her at least seventy-year-old father and his brothers or cousins maybe, I think, but not her own brothers. She must've been running away from a whole clan when she escaped to the squat. What should I say if I call, though? How should I introduce myself? Explain myself? And what for? This is when I grew afraid that her parents would remember the young boy, having had the opportunity to meet him once themselves.

27

While waiting for a connection worthy of the name of love, he hadn't counted on its quick manifestation in a racing heart and fingers nervously drumming on armrests. Only later did he read in all the books that love not only 'tore up reason and caused spiritual possession' as Ibn 'Arabi warned but that it also meant 'a wasting away', 'thoughts doggedly turning in circles, anxiety, sleeplessness, the burning desire, the fire of passion and being awake all night'. And that's not all: 'What's more, love causes abnormal behaviour, and causes one to lose their composure and grow childish.' Of course the young boy thought her not being there had to do with him, only with him and, therefore, didn't even consider the possibility that the most beautiful one could have been ill or overslept, or that she could simply have lost the desire to join the blockaders at the Ministry. Not even for the length of a bus ride was she ready to sit next to him again. Not even the fight against nuclear armament was important enough to her to be able to face him. Not even the revolutions of the time were big enough to make his suffering appear negligible. Like hieroglyphs the Autobahn signs blurred past his eyes, the announcements the poseur called on the microphone of the coach sounded like they'd been written in a foreign language. Arriving in the capital, the boy left the bus like a condemned man and let himself be led by the others as if going to his own execution. Though, in spite of their age, the others seemed as excited as Boy Scouts on an adventure, together with Majnun the boy would've been able to answer that he was just an old pack-donkey battered and bruised beneath the weight of his load: 'My body is thin and weak and still I have to carry my heavy load every day. And as soon as someone takes away my packsaddle to let me rest, innumerable horseflies besiege me and bite my wounds so that I call out: If only you hadn't allowed me to rest!' I have no memory of the actual blockade, nor how long it lasted. I only remember how the boy flew into a rage when two helmeted, and thanks to their body armour, giant-like police officers grabbed him under the armpits to carry him off. As if it were a case of life or death or as if he, to keep to the metaphor, were the donkey that no longer wants to be beaten, he screamed as if on a spit, kicked his arms and legs and, as the two police had bound his hands, made himself as stiff as a board before suddenly shaking his body as wildly as he could so that two more officers ran over and grabbed his feet. As a result, he was the only blockader from his town who wasn't put over on the lawn by the ramp to the Ministry but—despite the touching attempts of the poseur begging the police to arrest him instead of an innocent kid—carried straightaway to the green police wagon. That stated, the demonstration against nuclear armament had *really* turned into a disaster by the time his father picked him up from the police station in the capital that night. All the same, the images of the blockaders running riot which were shown on the evening news (you can still find the scenes today on YouTube, you just have to type 'Hardthöhe 1983' and 'blockade'), did not seem to have any noticeable effect on the solidarity the peace movement received within the power apparatus. Of course, the process of nuclear armament wasn't hindered in any way either.

28

'In truth, love is only a malady,' Ahmad Ghazali recognized and, being a realist to boot, added: 'Discretion and peace are foreign to it, are only on loan, for, in truth, love is division and duality and only in the fleeting moment of coupling unity. The rest is fantasy, and has nothing whatsoever to do with union.'

29

The reader who has already followed me for twenty-nine days will no doubt finally like to learn how the boy managed to win the most beautiful of all hearts in West Germany which beat for peace. At the same time, he or she will have to admit it would've been too melodramatic for the two of them to kiss at a demonstration during a battle with police or inside a prison yard. In reality, things are always a lot more normal, and long-winded too, than a fifteen-year-old makes them out to be, which is why the reader may have to wait until tomorrow for the kiss (I've come up with a plan envisioning ten pages for each stage of love—the meeting, the getting to know each other, the first caress and so on—so that the tale of such a great love can be told in one hundred days; up to page forty, I will talk about their coming together and up to page fifty, the state mystics refer to as 'self-annihilation and remaining' so that at least half of the story remains for despair). After the return trip with his father, the next storm broke the following morning when, right at the beginning of the first hour, the headmaster called him into his office. 'Not only did you take part in an illegal blockade—we'll talk about what non-violent means another time, my boy!' the headmaster said, seemingly close to getting physical himself. 'Not only did you protest against the state, the whole world saw it on the nightly news!' the headmaster thundered, grabbing his forehead. 'Not only did you cause your parents distress but you were audacious enough to have your mother drive you to the meeting point!' the headmaster continued, shaking his head. 'No, on top of it all, you skipped school! For that offence, at any rate, you will pay dearly,' the headmaster announced, who did not seem to have much faith in either the severity of the judiciary or the educational duties of the boy's parents. 'What does that mean exactly?' the boy asked sheepishly. 'The class conference shall decide!' the headmaster replied, directing him out of the office. The reader will be able to imagine how the boy felt as he slunk back into his classroom, and how awful he must have felt during the remaining double period. All things considered, however, the headmaster's threat seemed the most harmless. Even the ostracism of the various peace groups, which at the latest he'd encounter the following week, hardly bothered him; his parents' shame the least of all.

What weighed upon him more heavily than earthly or heavenly punishment combined, what depressed him at that moment in the classroom as much as it had the day before at police headquarters was the question as to why the most beautiful one had not travelled with them to the capital. But the moment she spoke to him for the second time in the smoking area he immediately forgot all the gods in heaven and all the heavenly creatures of earth. She'd actually overslept. And she hadn't seen the news the night before either.

30

I can hardly remember the days, if they weren't in fact weeks, that followed; nevertheless, despite the whims of memory, I cannot simply skip over them even if the kiss, which I wanted to arrive at today at the latest, now has to come a page later. I still know that, in a very casual way, the most beautiful girl in the whole schoolyard said to the boy that, if he was around and had time, he should come by to see her at the bar where she worked, and that that same night there he was standing out in front. They met a few afternoons, once for ice cream because the weather was slowly getting better (that is, as long as I'm not erroneously transferring later scenes to earlier dates), and once he even walked her to the doorstep of the squat she and her friends had occupied in order to block the construction of the city expressway. However, by no means had she fallen in love with a bang like he had. Four important years older, it would have been diffi-cult for her to reciprocate the feelings of a young boy who was still too young for the smoking area. Whenever possible, he took advantage of the all-round scorn for the secondary virtues that she, as a squatter, possessed; in this particular case, the protection of minors. He didn't impose; from one day to the other he was, no, not quiet, but inspired and already thanking the skies. By then he had long sensed that something big was coming, and did not want to jeopardize it with his impatience. Had he foreseen just how quickly that big thing would perish, he certainly would not have waited. That too belongs to the peculiarities that memory produces like the images of a roughly censored film: when I really think about it, the time in between their first date and their first kiss—in terms of days—must have been longer than the duration of their relationship, and all the same I almost forgot. It seems really short to me, while every minute of their rapture as well as their misery, both before and after, like an independent novel. That's not fair of my memory; it doesn't do us any favours by blocking out the moments in-between, underestimating the inconspicuous and tender. Although it bothers you in the present, those are the moments you most want to remember in the future.

31

They didn't kiss, but were kissed. That's how they both saw and even spoke about it. The two of them experienced something; in the blink of an eye, they experienced the same thing, and that's where they saw the wonder you encounter in telefilms. And yet, I'd be lying if I rewrote it, if I allowed for the possibility that both of their impressions were, in part, manufactured by the TV. But isn't it also the other way around? Doesn't what we perceive to be trivial for being reproduced *en masse* itself reproduce a basic experience that most of us had as kids? And furthermore, could the triviality of those very telefilms (and novels and blockbusters, etc.) not come from the fact that they take the specificity, not to mention stereotypes, of youthful love—which realists like Ibn 'Arabi well knew—and ham-handedly generalize and extend them to adult life? And last but not least: within the reluctance or fascination those same telefilms (and novels and blockbusters, etc.) provoke, don't we sense where we know the original from? At any rate, the shore upon which from one breath to the next they stood across from each other underwent a metamorphosis, nothing idyllic at all, just a little stretch of unpaved dirt between the warehouse of a shipping company and the car park of a home improvement store, neither daybreak nor a starry night sky, the moment their questioning glances and calling lips finally came together was simply during the second of two long breaks—though it just occurs to me that dull realism is often used for contrast in telefilms. Be that as it may, the kiss lasted longer than directors, novelists and producers ever estimate because they don't know about the gap in her teeth—even if it was only a few millimetres deep—his tongue pushed through. And if she hadn't already been prepared, at the latest she would've fallen in love when he showed up again, beaming enthusiastically in such a childlike and almost triumphant way.

32

As I said, I only sense what the most beautiful one liked about the boy and the hypothesis that his child-like enthusiasm and almost triumphant smile moved her is not based on any actual indications, that is, on anything she said, I mean, no one particular glance or reaction. No doubt she talked about the reasons for her affection or reciprocated a few of the boy's compliments, it's just that, no matter how favourably I try to lay it out for myself, I seem to have forgotten this aspect of their encounter completely. And what's more, I'm afraid that he only granted their experience so much attention because it suited his wishes. That the only reason he wanted her love was so that his own would be met. 'Lovers imagine their love to be attached to the figure of the beloved,' Ibn 'Arabi once remarked, 'but this is not so; it is only what drives them to meet and see the other. Were lovers to love the person or the existence of the beloved as such, which is to say, their personality, how they are independent from the lover and how they seek bliss, there would be no profit.' I can still remember how surprising it was that their lips felt so simultaneously smooth and soft, as if their surface were nothing but a film, their substance liquid. I'd still recognize the flavour of her lip balm even thirty years later, and in the chemist I never walk by the shelves with all the skin cream without keeping an eye out for the brand she used: in my mind I can smell her still. Together with their lips I can still remember the press of their sweaters, and the magnificent shockwaves her truly very hard breasts set loose in his head. I can also still remember how he was careful not to bump against her fly with his own, less she notice how suddenly the fabric had swollen. If I concentrated for a few minutes, I could come up with at least a hundred more of these completely banal impressions you never see in TV films (or novels, blockbusters, etc.), which, in their rare density, turn infatuation into a condition that doesn't appear to me any more sublime than the usual state of being, simply more concentrated, more concentrated on a self. In the best of cases I can assume or, rather, only suspect, which images flashed through her consciousness, and wonder if there were as many as through his. In their counterpart, lovers see only their own wishes and fears. As to the fact that she could just as well have looked off to the side in boredom—well, his eyes were closed. But she could have sweat, shook, moaned heatedly or defensively, and even flailed her hands in the air and he wouldn't have noticed a thing. I don't believe that such extreme insensibility at precisely that moment you have the most sensations is only to be attributed to that age one usually describes as a search for the self. 'In reality, no lover loves the beloved for the sake of the beloved's self,' Ibn 'Arabi adds, 'but solely for the sake of one's own. This is the truth without any doubt!'

33

There are also exceptions. Enlightened ones like Rabia al-Adawiyya, for example, who in the eighth century walked through Basra with a pail of water in one hand and a torch in the other. Whenever someone asked her what the pail and torch meant she answered: 'I want to put out the fires of hell and incinerate paradise so that God will be loved for His eternal beauty alone.'

34

As uplifting, electrifying, gigantic, etc. as the kiss was, just a few minutes later the boy was plagued by doubts as to whether their relationship could thereby be considered official. He did not simply wish to be with her, he wanted everyone to see that they were together too. From a mystical point of view, such vanity would certainly cast him down to one of the lowest rungs of love (though love it did remain, seeing as that it would be denied to him by the most beautiful girl in the whole schoolyard later on). After the kiss, for a long time they simply observed each other—he grinning as if having pulled off some kind of trick, she either tenderly or carefully depending on how you wanted to interpret it—then suddenly turned around and walked back to their respective classes without another word. The impulse to let go of each other before reaching the path came from her, as unnoticeably as ever, and she was the one who walked straight through the smoking area though the students were crowded together side by side which meant that the bell—strangely enough—could not yet have rung. But a lot of time had in fact passed, the boy thought as he and the most beautiful one wound their way through the smokers. Indeed, he'd gone through so many states, I think, both since and during the time he saw that black glow behind his closed eyelids. Only once they were twenty, thirty metres away from the smoking area did the two of them stop at that point where their paths diverged. Though her affection—when I call the glance back into mind today—could have been inscribed clearly enough in her smile, the boy could no longer conceal the questioning, maybe even imploring look in his own eyes. Wasn't it pain he could see in her face, pity that she'd soon have to hurt him? He almost grabbed her hand in front of the other *Abiturienten*, which he realized just before succumbing to the silent good-bye. In the entranceway, his pulse rate shot up, sweat broke out across his forehead as if he were getting ill, and on the stairs he grew so dizzy that he had to hold on to the railing. All those days he'd been at peace, certain of her love; down at the river, he'd even imagined himself to be in that condition of delirious happiness considered impossible on earth, where creation, as promised, was neither broken nor even cracked. And that was why the fear that she'd only allowed the tenderness by mistake, in a moment she already regretted, took hold of him all the more terribly. Though thirty years later I think a whole lot must've gone through their heads on the stairs and in the hallways to their respective classrooms, the idea of already pushing him away just after kissing him couldn't have been one of them. The boy, on the other hand, felt it was such a great danger that he remained, shall we say, fixated: like being convinced you'll get a failing mark in maths. From one second to the next, he interpreted all of the most beautiful one's movements in the worst possible way, each and every gesture, all the unstated words, and even the movement of her lips when they kissed, that kiss which had been so uplifting, electrifying and so on. During the short break when his classmate asked if everything was OK he stuttered a curt 'no'.

35

'Everything now depends on the next time we see each other,' the boy thought, and jumped up as soon as the bell for the long break rang. The teacher insisted that class was only over when he said it was over and asked the boy to sit down, but the boy wasn't listening any more or was but didn't care, and flew up from the last row of chairs past the lectern and out through the door so that the teacher, thinking he understood what was wrong, called after him asking whether he really had to go that badly. No doubt the rest of the class began to laugh, but the boy really didn't hear anything at all any more. He'd already disappeared into the hall and, despite his Birkenstocks, took the stairs three at a time prior to running straight across the courtyard to the smoking area. Refusing to hide behind any shoulders, he began to cast grim then evermore doubtful glances at the *Abiturienten* coming in one after the other then commenced walking back and forth as if a supervisor himself. Before the bell rang a second time, he left the smoking area to look for the most beautiful one, his mind so sharp that he marked all of her possible whereabouts on a site plan so that he could go through them one by one. When the bell rang, he didn't go back to class, but gaspingly walked to the stairwell where she'd most likely appear; after that, he followed the last students onto one of the upper floors where he imagined the *Abiturienten* had their lessons and looked into all the classrooms that still had their doors open, accepting the confused looks of the teachers walking in. He spent the rest of the period for the first time on the riverbank alone.

36

‘God made Adam aware of all His names without exception and that the Creator can be praised through every name in creation. Adam thereby celebrated the greatness and magnificence of God.’ Ibn ‘Arabi then adds that sentence which could double as an introduction to a history of world literature: ‘No name is meaningless, not even the name of a large or small dish, which differs from the opinion of those who understand nothing of the greatness of things.’ An anecdote from the ninth-century Egyptian mystic Dhū-I-Nūn could also apply. Someone once said to him: ‘Show me the largest name of God!’ To which Dhū-I-Nūn replied: ‘Show me the smallest!’ and threw the man out.

37

With the most casual expression his quivering lips would allow him to muster, he sat down on a stool at the bar in the early evening and stayed there until closing time shortly after one. Of course he should've been home long ago, but so what. His father could have been sitting on a stool next to him and he wouldn't have noticed. The glances the most beautiful one gave him every time she came by the bar to pick up drinks, the five, six displays of affection they exchanged during her shift removed all doubt that her kiss that morning had been anything other than a mistake. She seemed to avoid any conversation; as opposed to the other two earlier, still innocent evenings he'd visited her at work, the opportunity didn't arise too often and then only in passing, barely longer than a minute. Already upon saying hello he'd announced his intention to wait for her and did not show his surprise when she did not object. I don't think the scriptures are more meaningful, more fascinating, or more mysterious to the believer than the time she got off work was to the boy—in fact, let's have another look at those promises. The Quran, for example, which describes paradise even more extensively than the Bible, talks about multiple gardens, sometimes four, sometimes only two, 'beneath which rivers flow' and where the inhabitants are 'adorned with bracelets of gold, and wear green garments, while reclining upon thrones'. Naturally, there's milk and honey too. Moreover, it mentions the graceful sounds which caress their ears; and lists the various types of trees beneath which they rest as well as thornless lote trees and acacia trees rich with leaves; the vaunted palaces where they live and the exalted thrones upon which they recline; the silver vessels, gold bowls and crystal goblets; and, finally, the delicacies which please their palates, above all dates and grapes and, for the sake of variety, the flesh of fowl and that wine which neither intoxicates nor goes bad as well as other drinks containing ginger too; it even mentions the comfortable climate, and for desert dwellers the shade is emphasized. But, to be rather blunt about it, what is all that indeed compared to the joys the boy imagined to himself while sitting on his barstool? No, that lay ahead in five, four, three, two and finally just one hour? He for his part would not have wanted to trade a single kiss much less a glimpse and then caress of her naked body for any music of the spheres, food and drink, jewellery or good climatic conditions. The Quran comes closer to the boy's situation when it promises the believer 'all that souls desire and eyes find sweet' and when it describes with almost unbelievable clarity at the beginning of Surah 56, for example, the sexual promise of those wide-eyed houris like pearls in shells, when the inhabitants of heaven hear no vain talk nor sinful speech but 'only the saying "Peace! Peace!"' That stated, the music in the bar was pretty good too.

38

The reader will have difficulty believing that I've been writing about the boy's great love for thirty-eight days now without having once remembered the journals lying in the chest with the letters, or will believe it only because the sudden disclosure of an authentic source seems far too contrived for a story to really be contrived. All the same, it won't matter what the reader thinks about the introduction of the journals as they prove to be unrewarding and even embarrassingly banal right away. The title alone —'Dream and Chaos'—announced to posterity in calligraphic script on the cover sets the tone of pubescent self-embellishment that exasperatingly appears on almost every single page. To me it seems to be an unconscious caricature of the Sturm-und-Drang writers whose sacralization of one's own mood must have had an effect on the boy on multiple levels. Of their originality and linguistic brilliance, however, not a trace remained save a lot of exclamation marks: 'What a beautiful feeling it is to be in love!!!' What's more, there's the subjective impression of being the first person to set foot on a new continent, an impression which, in reality, the world is already quite familiar with. He called her Fay, Little Fay, and the Fairy, a name which had never even occurred to the authors of the corniest scripts. Depictions of concrete situations I could use for my story, though, are nowhere to be found. It's almost as if the boy wanted to write pure, downright insubstantial poetry; there are very few tips to help me reconstruct the way things unfolded. He only seems to mention stomach aches (which, of course, are notorious in pop *Schlager* too), stomach aches or butterflies, a racing heart, general agitation. It shocked me to see how little originality we grant that very day we're convinced of experiencing something unique. I was confronted by a similar sense of disillusionment just a few years ago when I tried to go to marriage counselling, an experience which only led to the understanding that our perceptions, reactions, behavioural patterns, misunderstandings, erotic phases and self-perception corresponded precisely to the model predefined by our social status, age, length of the relationship, number of children and so on. If it hadn't been over already, that shock of self-recognition would have administered the *coup de grâce* to my marriage. Having said that, the mystical experience is also categorizable and, therefore, by no means individualistic, otherwise the mystics would not have established such an exact and psychologically sophisticated system of reference points and conditions through which one's inner life becomes the scene of revelation. The reason I nevertheless mention the diary is because I can then quickly put it back in the chest—although the idea that someone else could read it, even if only my own son making his way through my estate, is horrific, something keeps me from simply throwing it away. After all, it is a sign of life and was at one time extremely important to me—the reason I mention it is the discovery that the great love my memory has made such a fuss about, from the first kiss to the break-up, did not even last a week. The pain of separation, of course, lasted much longer. In some ways, I still feel it today. For if I didn't, I wouldn't be telling our story at all.

39

He followed her silently as she said goodbye to the bar owner and the few remaining guests still sitting at the counter and then out on the sidewalk. Her car turned out to be rather normal, a gift from her parents I imagine, no hand-painted Citroën Duck or convertible VW Beetle, which would have been in line with the strict tastes of the radical *Autonome* of the time. And yet, he didn't find the Opel Ascona or her reminder to 'buckle up' bourgeois. During the trip, he didn't dare turn his head to even look at the stick shift as factories which thirty years earlier had still been active drifted past them on the right or later the warehouses, wholesalers and after a while, the railway lines (practically speaking, they took the industrial road, it just went straight through the city centre). Traffic light to traffic light he inched ever-closer to his paradise and yet remained worried as to whether he needed to come up with some kind of clever or, even better, poetic topic to talk about so that she, God forbid, would not think of dropping him off at home. Thankfully, nothing came to him that was any more stimulating than silence. Behind the railway station, which lay in the same darkness as the factories, warehouses and wholesalers, the most beautiful one parked her car and turned to look at him expectantly. It took a few seconds for the boy to understand that he needed to get out for her to lock the passenger-side door. At last he was standing in front of that row of houses whose demolition she would protest as unsuccessfully as he had against nuclear armament. Thanks to the word-painted bed-sheets hanging down from the windows it was easy to figure out in which one of them she lived. To his surprise, it was also the only one in which a light still quite literally burned: in the kitchen, the members of the resistance were sitting around with red wine and hash, all seven of them even older than the most beautiful girl in the whole schoolyard, which is to say, truly grown-up. If the two of them sat down, that much he understood, they wouldn't be getting up too quickly and early in the morning he had class (which, of course, he'd skip without thinking twice but, perhaps, so close to her exams, she wouldn't). Furthermore, he was worried about how he'd hold up (and everything depended on it); he'd never had that many beers in a single evening before and that wasn't counting all the sleepless nights over the past few days, all the excitement—purely unfavourable circumstances to reveal the Arcanum that the union of two bodies was to him. The conceivable question as to whether he'd ever slept with a woman caused his lips to once again begin quivering. In her veins, on the contrary, the blood seemed to be flowing as calmly as the little river next to which they had kissed for the first time; she wasn't in any hurry and had no need to communicate to him how the rest of the night would unravel. She surely had enough experience. Thirty years later, I suspect the reason she left silently, sat in the car silently, went up the stairs ahead of him silently, and avoided every glance was that she herself was unsure what to do with the boy who for whatever reasons still attracted her though he wasn't even old enough to be in the smoking area. What's a bit trickier to understand: In the stairwell did she consider taking him up for wine and hash in the kitchen or for going to her room? Either way, to the boy she seemed like a priestess who would only decide at the last moment whether or not to grant him access to the holy mysteries.

40

Were I to follow the plan I so carelessly mentioned earlier, I'd have to speak about their union by today at the latest. That alone, I now realize, consists of so many pages that I'd like to think about it for more than just one day, let's say, ten times as many. Compositional considerations, of course, would also suggest a prolongation of the event in order to have it smack in the middle of the story. The 'self-annihilation and remaining' would slip a page later but still leave forty for despair. And so today, instead of rushing right through their coming together, I'd merely conclude with what in all religious traditions precedes the experience of the saint by explaining—yet again in the words of Ibn 'Arabi—what was holy about two young people consummating their love in the spring of 1983 in a small West German town. 'Man will never be able to see God without an intermediary,' he wrote in *The Ringstones of Wisdom*, 'for God, in his absolute essence, is independent of all worlds. But as divine reality in its essence is inaccessible and can only be contemplated within a substance, the contemplation of God is the strongest and most complete in women; and the most powerful union of all is the sexual one.'

41

The room: a dorm-like mattress draped with Indian-looking scarves where three or even four people slept or more likely turned night into day. Three fruit crates of thin plywood with her favourite books, textbooks and records. No desk for her to do her homework but a tower made out of a cassette deck, a radio, an amplifier and a record player, to the left and right two self-assembled, moss-green painted speakers which at the same time served as the place for the incense (the left) and the ashtray (the right). Untreated softwood shelves for make-up, primarily all-natural cosmetics, pens, notebooks and various other utensils. On the once-beige-but-now-stained carpet stacks or, rather, piles of clothes and a red-varnished chair as a clothes rack. On top and below the two windowsills a host of empty wine bottles from whose necks candles towered like ballerinas. The walls were painted a fire yellow and decorated with a poster of a jazz festival as well as one of Picasso's dove of peace which at that time in West Germany hung in the rooms of hundreds of thousands of high-schoolers, university students and squatters. Last but not least, six man-sized potted plants that today would make you think of a hothouse. In short, a room that not only promised the discovery of love or corresponded to the boy's ideals of interior design down to the smallest details including the terracotta tea set but one that transcended taste and desire altogether and stood for nothing less than a political utopia. That, exactly like that, was how he wanted to live just once, just as 'wild and dangerously' as a post-card pinned to the door recommended a certain Arthur do. Although the postcard was even more common among high-schoolers, university students and squatters than Picasso's *Dove of Peace*, I never asked myself just who that Arthur might have been. Schopenhauer? I already know that nothing from that time has stuck in the collective memory. As dramatic, subversive, indeed apocalyptic as the fight against nuclear armament had seemed to those who gathered together in mass demonstrations in the former capital, formed human chains across Autobahns, blockaded military barracks or handed out roses to helmeted police officers armed with truncheons, how quickly the West German peace movement fizzled out without a trace when what was known as the Double-Track Decision was eventually pushed through. And today historians even credit the Double-Track Decision with the fall of the Wall! Nevertheless, I still treasure that time which, at best, people still remember for its curious fashions, its knitting men and shapelessly dressed women; nevertheless, the more I think about it, the more I treasure it because there is one thing it most certainly wasn't, namely, cool and ironic. As in the traditions my story is connected to but for the last time in the Western world, things like wanting the best for others, gentleness, altruism and even weakness were considered virtues. As mirrored in the Warsaw Pact, the words of the barefooted ninth-century saint Bishr ibn al-Hareth that you are incomplete so long as your worst enemy remains vulnerable before you, could have been uttered in the Protestant Students' Union. Soft water breaks the hardest stone and so on, everything has been refuted, everything seems to come from the day before yesterday or even prehistory, and yet, deep down, I still believe in it all today, if for different historical reasons. Without the fire of love as a political message—which lit up once more ten or fifteen years after the hippies—the most beautiful girl in the whole schoolyard would never have offered the holiest of mysteries to that scarecrow of a beau. For it is becoming more and more clear to me that her surprising affection was also based on an idea of emancipation, to pique the guys' interest, to appreciate the unsuspecting nature of naivety and to see a certain strength even in vulnerability. And once in love with him, she seemed to have decided to introduce him to the discovery of two bodies in this way so that the fire would burn inside of him for the rest of his life. What leads me to think so? Well, she never asked him if he'd already slept with a girl. She just knew as she lit the candles, which then began to dance in the bottlenecks, one after the other.

42

I wonder if things will go the same way for my son as they did for the boy when he saw a woman naked and stretched out on a bed for the first time, the two wave-like lines her slender body made, her thighs pressed together as if still in doubt but her lips open and revealing the Eleusinian gap between her teeth, her taut breasts likewise quivering from excitement with their little towers rising up as if made of brick, one hand on her stomach, the other to the side to welcome him in an embrace, nothing shaved—that wasn't normal back then, it would've been seen as unnatural and traditionalist—her genitals, legs, underarms and even armpits a heavenly garden of meadows and woods . . . I wonder if things even *could* go the same way for my son. It's not as if the boy had never seen a naked woman in films or at Baggersee Lake; changing your shirt, trousers and underwear out in the open was considered good form by the protestors, especially if you'd been soaked by a water cannon, say, or were ostentatiously and shamelessly sunbathing in the Hofgarten of the former capital, or if during a march you'd stopped to squat and pee by the side of the road, the women I mean, though naturally there were some men who squatted out of solidarity, too. But this was different. In those kinds of situations there was no erotic charge (even if now and again the boy had pointed at the women). It was more a sense of unspoilt nature, and it virtually negated the sexual, dismissed it as a form of repression one had overcome. I can hardly remember instances of nudity for the sake of stimulation; as I said, it was frowned upon within the movement but it doesn't seem to have been omnipresent throughout society, in general, before the introduction of cable TV. Then again, maybe the boy had just been watching the wrong programmes. Either way, there was also the fact that the town they lived in was not only small but also characterized by a particularly strict interpretation of Protestantism and most homes were ruled, at the very least, by a strict sense of morals which had all but disappeared in the rest of the country after the sexual revolution. Homosexuality—to give just one example—was more than just indecent; even to a boy who was used to seeing women he didn't know pee it seemed unthinkable or at most something that happened in the land of his favourite writers, though even there he had to be hit on the nose before understanding that indeed they meant love between two men. And lastly, one still wasn't familiar with, and least of all within the peace movement, that pressure for flawlessness, for perfection, and the total preparation of the body which in the meantime has begotten, even in small, strictly Protestant towns, a regime—who am I kidding?—a totalitarianism of seduction. For what other reason than total exhibitionism is it then that every muscle has to be trained, every spare hair ripped out of the body, and even one's buttocks tattooed when the most beautiful girl of a West German school in 1983 'had absolutely no need of make-up' as the poet Nizami wrote about the legendary Layla, 'for even the milk she drank turned the colour of roses upon her cheeks and lips and with lustrous eyes and beauty mark her mother had brought her into the world'? Whereas on his mobile alone my son could have saved more pornography than his father ever ... God help me! Now I sound just like my own father and probably all my forefathers before him who perceived the decline of morals, especially in the heydays of literature, to be marked by a loss of nuances, impoverishment through abundance, disorientation through directness, stupor through excitation. The dialectic of the veil, which is key to Sufism: God laid the curtains and partitions upon Majnun's path so that from day to day his eye would mature until it became attentive enough to see Layla. And so as little as my father and my forefathers I, too, doubt my son will ever experience a similar sensation as the boy who stood silently before the mattress for one, then two, then three minutes before finally tearing off his clothes.

43

'Someone sees all your genitals,' wrote Baha al-Din Walad (whose son Rumi today is revered by the likes of the pop singer Madonna) in the thirteenth century, 'someone sees your nakedness, your member, just as a wife sees her husband and a husband his wife for the first time. They see all of their beloved's secret places and shameful things; they enjoy each other, let themselves go in front of each other, and are uninhibited. And so you, too, should throw yourself uninhibitedly before God, who sees all of your secret parts and your nakedness, and say: O Lord, rule over my little parts, as you always do, for not one can hide itself before you.'

44

Thirty years later, I know that it was clear to her from the very beginning that she'd have to introduce him to the act of love even though to the boy—who with a jump not dissimilar to a plunge fell over her just to all of a sudden ask himself how one swam—it wasn't. No doubt he'd imagined all possible permutations of the situation over the last few days and, above all, the course of the evening while sitting at the bar and had prepared his mind for every movement, sequence of motions and possible position. But now that his body was actually on top of hers and his member, to stay with the designation, was unintentionally brushing her pubic hair, he was terrified as to how he might survive the next five seconds without emptying himself at the wrong place and the wrong time. He quickly raised his buttocks and began to kiss her in the idiotic hope that his excitement would subside so long as he kept his privates far enough away from hers; then, with the same logic, he knelt down next to her, and raced up and down her body with all ten fingers and mouth like a cleaning crew careening down the hallway that connected the two buildings of the *Gymnasium*. That body which was still so delightful and which somehow—this presumptuousness and sense of superiority made his offence significant—belonged to him, was subject to him, was his to possess, had turned into an unfamiliar piece of material. *It* or, rather, she did not respond to any of his caresses with a movement suggesting pleasure; on the contrary, it or she shocked him through the appearance of lifelessness. This farce of an act of foreplay cannot have lasted too long (today I'd guess not even sixty seconds) before the most beautiful one sat up—I'd love to see the look on her face: Was she chuckling? Groaning?—took his hands, and placed them on her thighs in order to start over with the proverbial ABCs. To the boy, however, that minute seemed like an eternity in which God, as the Sufis would say, had left him alone with his Self. This is a moment of panic that can occur before the lover realizes that desire is not the goal, but to be desired. The guides describe this as the beginning of knowledge. In ideal cases, before the stretch of annihilation begins, reverence follows terror, to be followed by exaltation, then awe. As for the boy, that terror remained so powerful that his arousal was deflated until further notice.

45

Sahl al-Tustari, banished to Basra in 874 CE, was asked: 'What should one think of a man who maintains he is like a door that only moves when someone moves him?' 'Only one of two kinds of men would say such a thing,' Sahl answered. 'A true believer or a heretic.'

46

'Be authentic!' she urged him as his fingers fluttered clumsily across her thighs. And regardless of whatever books had put those words in her mouth— feminist theory, psychology, liberation theology —they had to have been inspired by God, for they cut through the boy with a plausibility normally reserved for divine revelations. I surmise that when the boy heard the catchword 'authenticity' (something he probably did not totally understand and a term which today still turns my stomach) the night took that shift thanks to which it became the celebration he'd been thinking about the whole evening or really the whole day (when, not to say, all the previous days combined) since coming across her illuminated on the rock, before her the little, prosaic river with the four-lane road on the other side, behind her a bonfire site littered with empty beer cans and sausage packets, as a backdrop the parked lorries of the shipping company. If at least I'd come across the words 'be yourself!' or even better 'just be now!' in my journal, I could live with it, I could even find some wisdom in what's there. But no, she said: 'Be authentic!' Of all things, 'authentic'. I now remember she probably even repeated the word, which must have been in fashion thirty years ago and even earlier in bigger towns. And yet, it had no more effect than a guide's words: it neither added to nor diminished the experience, it merely reorganized everything. I surmise that from that moment on—hands on his thighs, authenticity in his ear—the boy no longer did what he'd intended to do, no longer strove for that one goal. 'OK,' he stuttered, simply 'OK', a term that didn't sound any better than her own.

47

I don't remember and, what's more, can't find anything in the journal about how his fingers crept, flew, hurried, dashed, pounced, floated, or were conjured back to her body, her ribs, or maybe even her shoulders. Be that as it may, I'd like to rescue the next moment from oblivion: that curious, to him elegant, almost artistic-seeming half-twist-like movement with which their upper bodies fell onto the Indian-looking scarves in such a perfect way that, without a jerk or a twitch, they ended up lying next to each other in an embrace, his left leg curved around her thigh, their mouths so close he could feel her breath on the end of his nose, his penis relaxed against her pubic hair, her chest nestled against his own, softer than any cushion. And I believe that whether because of the movement, the breath on the tip of his nose, the shrivelled remains of his excitement, or wanting to get her to laugh so that he could see the gap between her teeth, he was the one, the boy, who began to grin and she, who he quickly declared the most beautiful creature on earth, smiled and broke into a similarly amused grin before both of them collapsed with—no, not resounding but sparkling, bubbly—laughter, a kind of giggling that rippled in ever-greater waves through their bodies before they bent into each other snorting, his forehead pressed into her lap, her chin on his back. And though once they'd started they didn't immediately stop, they attempted to change their position to get some air and grab their stomachs. And so they untangled themselves from each other and found themselves once again side by side on their backs, in a strange way each for themselves, but without feeling any kind of separation. Gradually their muscles relaxed, their stomachs stopped hurting and their laughter turned into a kind of pant before dying out in two sighs. To ensure that she wouldn't dissolve into air or run off to the toilet, he grabbed her hand and, reassured, felt his own bliss. Just who had initiated that movement, whether it had been him or her, not even God in his omniscience would have been able to say. Baha al-Din Walad calls the flow of wine, that is, love, one of the four rivers of paradise which God allows to flow through every body. The other three being the honey flow of joy between compatible couples, the milk flow of sympathy between human beings, and the water flow of life and knowledge.

48

Were I from now on to follow the plan I've already amended once, I'd have to complete the first part of the story—their union—on page fifty in order to finally recount the bit about annihilation and remaining. That way all the despair—if no longer half of my story—could at least suggestively take on the magnitude that the journal grandiloquently offers it over the course of the months to follow. But that's ridiculous. The journal doesn't adequately depict the relationships as, little by little, it gripes about other experiences, incidents and even before the year's out a new affair until the most beautiful one—who left his world as soon as she was done with her *Abitur*—only finds mention as a star which on particularly clear nights can be seen in the vault of the sky. Seen from outside, from the perspective of his fellow students, parents, or maybe even his son who'll come across the journal while settling my estate, the boy might give the impression that his love was only an episode and, in truth, as insignificant as her last or, rather, only letter charged. And yes, I admit, he did not turn into Majnun who only saw Layla in everything, who when seeing wild animals would cry out 'Layla!', who when seeing the mountains would cry out 'Layla!', who when looking at people would cry out 'Layla!', and when asked who he was would cry out 'Layla!'. If the boy's love had indeed reached that kind of intensity, today I could neither extol nor bemoan it as he would not have come back to that reality where one tells stories; he would have 'gone crazy', which is what the name 'Majnun' means (in a pathological sense, schizophrenic), and would likely be sitting in a mental institution, far from being revered like the love-crazed prince. As it turned out, after a brief illness the boy would return to school, not even two months later pass all his classes, four years after that complete his *Abitur*, go to university, establish a family, ruin a marriage and continue onwards along the typical paths of modern-day life so that thirty years later he could sit in a cosy study and remember that one time he, too, had lost his mind. An episode, true, but, in comparison to a lifetime, what is youthful infatuation other than an episode? Didn't Ibn 'Arabi also describe it as equivalent, as related, as corresponding to (and not only in its symptoms) the mystic's 'drowning' in the divine? Did he fail to see the difference? He had to have seen it. In addition to divine love, he suffered earthly love too. He writes about it in *Interpreter of Desires*, calling her the most beautiful one as well, and likewise he set out, studied, taught, and one day remembered it all in a study. The agony of the break-up only *seemed* to fade; in reality, however, it drove so deeply into his soul as both poison and healing potion that thereafter all seeking and, in particular, the search for the divine beloved, would be moved by a yearning again and again and then for even longer: he'd have to experience the dissolution that love is at its beginning and end for all eternity. More than any other Sufi who still wrote books perhaps, Ibn 'Arabi penetrated into the unknown along the narrow path of knowledge over-grown with delusions. I, on the contrary, have not travelled those roads which pave the tradition even once. Thus, the only comparison could be that of a bowl, which is also one of the names of God. In this sense, however (that of a bowl, I mean), the boy rightly argued that he had not been deeply in love with the most beautiful girl on earth, and the pain of the break-up as a poison and life elixir drove its way so deeply into my soul that all my seeking thereafter has only been that of longing. My original plan to dedicate half of my story to despair was a mistake.

According to that timeline, the relationship between fulfilment and need would be that between the number one and infinity, or if not infinity, then a week and the rest of one's life. It's just that I'm already talking about the forty-eighth day and still haven't made it to describing their union.

49

Medieval holy sheikhs also describe the relationship between earthly and divine love as a bridge and do not consider any student complete who has never loved another deeply. Fakhruddin Iraqi, a thirteenth-century philosopher and mystic from the western Iranian city of Hamedan, for example, who himself once followed a beloved all the way to the Indian city of Multan, tells the story of a novitiate who made his way through multiple forty-day retreats without achieving enlightenment. The novitiate's master then sent him to a wine tavern where he fell hopelessly in love with a beautiful woman or a young man. After taking all of love's ecstasies, pain and indignities upon himself, he returned, at last experienced, to his master. I don't want to say that I've ever stepped foot on the bridge. But I know the wine tavern very well indeed.

50

Where should I begin? How should I limit myself in order to live up to the explosion of impressions that union offered the boy in just one page? The fireworks of which he was not only observer but also the demolition expert? For authenticity's sake, at the latest when he—once more highly concentrated on giving her pleasure—penetrated her? If he could only gather his wits long enough, that'd already be something, he told himself and regretted all the wine they'd had since their laugh attack, and the joint they'd smoked together. What he didn't realize was that it was precisely that cloud which protected him, certainly when penetrating her, from losing it altogether. To his relief everything went quite well. 'Like clockwork,' he thought. I can still remember the expression, 'like clockwork', and the feeling of being enclosed. No, not only his member (to once and for all stick with the term that the well-deserving Orientalist Fritz Meier of Basel elegantly chose with a slight cough for his study of Baha al-Din Walad), but with my whole body and soul and everything that is—enclosed by her, subsumed within her. It really was a different kind of intoxication of the senses than the quick release he obtained beneath his own sheets. It was 'as when trees and plants draw up water and earth,' as Baha al-Din Walad himself describes carnal as well as religious lust, 'so that one could say: you draw on God, without a speech, a thought, or even a perception of an idea.' No, that wasn't the summit, but would almost have been one—too early, too deep, too short, just a hint and then gone—had the boy not propped himself on his hands and raised his upper body whereby his member, driving a little deeper into her, set loose new waves of pleasure that frightened him, that he didn't want, that he tried to get rid of with thoughts of the dentist in order not to lose control completely. He looked at her. How? That I don't know. It was me myself there, alarmed maybe, or confused too, at a loss for words or simply wondering what a wonderful, too wonderful thing this was, and so the boy decided for the time being not to move one single millimetre more. Just no more quakes! In the meanwhile, she didn't appear to be waiting on his next movement and, for the moment, seemed to be enjoying the delay, the staying still, the tension. She had her eyes closed and her lips open so wide that the gap between her teeth lay there unprotected. It became clear to him that, for the moment, there would be no further instructions from her end, and it's become clear to me that their union cannot only be told from one perspective.

51

‘God's organ takes many forms,’ Baha al-Walad knows. ‘It can take the form of a young woman and the desire for them which He has placed within men. Intercourse for men, as well as for male animals, comes from God touching them in the form of these women and girls, in the form of their acts, which is to say, their kisses and the like. God's organ can also take the form of men, as well as male animals, and it is in this way that God has intercourse with female beings and touches them, as He touched Mary and as good and bad spirits touch people. God's organ can take the form of green plants, water, air and earth. And no one knows the manner of such contact, touch or intercourse.’

52

Presumably, in spite of everything, it went too quickly for her. As much as he tried to further postpone climax—one can also say that his effort at that point was utterly and completely concentrated on minimizing his sexual pleasure—as carefully as he thus moved his backside he was at the same time aware that the ideal union was not supposed to resemble a balancing act and that female ecstasy was not going to come about in slow motion. But what could he do? Had he sped up just a little, his excitement would have got out of hand. Nonetheless, he remained full of passionate intensity and the process, I won't deny it—the back and forth, the up and down, the immerging into and emerging out of her body, which enveloped his member as tightly and softly as a fluid and, as a consequence, aroused all those associations with the sea though the boy had still not read anything about the shorelessness of which the mystics speak—was incredible. Or, well, it could have been if there hadn't been so much fear mixed up inside it all, the fear of failing in front of a creature who seemed as beautiful as the very creator himself. Interestingly enough, the mystics have nothing to say about that. Premature ejaculation does not appear in their use of metaphor; the comparison of such unfortunate, abruptly ended ecstasy, which had to have been an occurrence—whether caused by outer or inner disturbance—does not appear even once in the writings of Baha al-Walad who, while sacralizing sexual love, at the same time sexualized ritual: 'One could say that within the trap of a prayer you are lying on top of a real beauty and, with its verses, your lips are pressed against hers.' And this fact, that the greatest excitement lies just under the executioner's axe of early, far too early discharge, and can thus turn into its opposite, is more than simply mean, it's downright malicious. That stated, in other contexts the mystics by all means talk about balance. When they discuss the terrors of the experience of God and of the path as narrow as a razor's edge, to the left and right the abyss of irreversible separation—what is that if not a balancing act? They know that God has not arranged things to be as benign or achievable as they appear to lovers; they are familiar with God's malice and have written whole books about it. But they also maintain that no boy can take the path; for were he to do so, soon enough he would no longer be, well, a boy. He'd take on the features of an Ata as-Salimi, who to his contemporaries in the eighth century looked like a 'dried-out hose'. 'He seemed to be a man who was not from this world,' one reported. And another stated: 'Whenever I'd run into him, his eyes were overflowing. I could only compare him to a woman who has lost a child.' Every time Ata performed his ritual ablutions, he would violently tremble and cry. When someone asked him why, he said: 'I want to undertake a violent act: I want to stand before God in prayer.' So far, things were still going pretty well for the boy.

53

She, on the other hand—I can't seem to extract an expression, a gesture, a sound, from the moss of oblivion that would show how she felt when he finally began to move back and forth in a jerky motion just like he'd seen in films and even one time a lot more vigorously at Baggersee Lake. Most likely after a couple of seconds already—'Oh God!' he cried out in his head, and 'Shit, shit, shit!'—he lost control over his member which, after a few thrusts, more after-the-fact or even simulated than necessary, came. Though he'd meant to fill her innermost being completely, expand it even, from one moment to the next he seemed to be moving in the empty air or, more accurately, not moving but hanging there alone like a bent, leafless branch: indeed, after expansion comes constriction, *qabḍ wa-basṭ*. Thirty years later, the idea that her desire might have reached a summit or even only an edge, a crag, is ludicrous. Back then, however, that night—well, it was already early in the morning—in the fire-yellow room the boy was truly concerned as to whether he had brought her ecstasy or not. But, in the end, he didn't know what signs to look for and had shown his own far more unassumingly than in the films and at Baggersee Lake. Eyes still closed, lips opened a little, she kept him from immediately slipping out of her body by lightly pressing her fingers on his buttocks. At the same time, she rolled hers almost unnoticeably in every direction—maybe she'd been doing so the whole time—or really by only a few millimetres, and only so much so that once again a soft and for the boy somehow conciliatory friction was created; not a pleasant feeling, no, only a friction and through it, once again, a new kind of sensation. And then I must have fallen asleep.

54

'Wake up.' There was a painful throbbing against the inside of his forehead. At the same time, as if she'd sensed his headache, he felt her comforting hand on his hair. 'Wake up, we've got to go to school.' Already dressed, she sat on the edge of the mattress and with her other hand held out a handmade pottery cup. 'It's late.' He sat up only to be cast back onto the pillow by the throbbing that suddenly drove against his forehead from outside. Their outlines blurred, the fire-yellow walls seemed to waver, but that's not why he closed his eyes. It had a lot more to do with his concern of putting her off with a pained expression: admitting a low tolerance for alcohol and hash would once again have made his inexperience obvious. 'You've got to get up, it's late.' In the end, she didn't live so wildly and dangerously that, right before her *Abitur*, she was ready to skip class. Couldn't she just leave him in bed and come back in the afternoon, maybe with some rolls in her suede leather bag?

He'd do the washing up beforehand and greet her with coffee as if they lived together. In the middle of considering whether he could risk suggesting it, she kissed him on the mouth. 'Wake up.' That was it. That was the kiss. The next time he opened his eyelids, he was finally there again, could quite clearly see her nose—bent slightly upwards at the tip like a ski jump—her kind eyes, her hair falling onto her forehead with a single part, the gleam of her lip balm, the fire-yellow walls standing straight. Things still throbbed against or inside his head, but he didn't care. He almost enjoyed the pain as a result, a manifestation, a trophy of that glory which had finally been bestowed upon him with the kiss. 'Yeah, I'm coming,' he said and wrapped his arms around her neck to pull her down onto the mattress. 'The tea!' she cried laughing but letting him. One more spot on the carpet wouldn't make any difference.

55

He didn't risk kissing her goodbye in the entrance hall to the *Gymnasium*, he just waited anxiously to see if she'd display any sign of affection before he consented without complaint to her hurried 'Bye!' At the swing door leading to the rooms of the upper forms, she turned around with a smile that could have been just as affectionate as pitying. What did he really know about her final judgement of the night? His doubt had already returned earlier while brushing his teeth with his index finger. He hadn't yet made it to the other swing door when he heard a distinctly adult voice call his name: as it turned out, it was the school secretary angrily ordering him to the headmaster. I'd really like to know if my headmaster is still alive, if he ever happened upon the boy's name in the newspaper and since that time decided to follow him, maybe even read his books, maybe even *this* book, this sentence. He'd be ancient by now—in his grey and, despite his leanness, always-too-tight suits even thirty years ago he seemed thirty years too late. And on top of it he was short, as if he'd shrunk somehow, and his ties were too wide and his glance was always intensely strict. To be fair, he had his reasons to be worried about the boy who ever since the blockade of the Ministry of Defence had become a problematic case and had seemingly driven his parents to irrevocable madness: they'd called the school choking with tears to ask if their child had shown up. But, in retrospect, wouldn't the headmaster find it comical himself? How with the door still open he yelled so loud that even the *Abiturienten* upstairs had to have heard him. How he called him heartless, once again threatened him with expulsion and then the youth welfare office, and at one point even raised his hand to box the boy's ears so that he'd reveal where and, above all, with which one of the older students he'd spent the night. 'As if I didn't know already!' the headmaster yelled, his index finger shaking as he went after the boy like a felon. 'As if the whole school didn't know where you've been spending your breaks as of late!' No doubt he'd laugh about the scene which, despite all the other problem cases, he can't have forgotten and shake his head recalling the unconstitutional conspiracy he suspected the boy of being involved with. For me, on the contrary, the anxiety, rage and defiance came so tangibly into my conscience when writing it was as if just yesterday I was still that boy. And how proud I am still, thirty years later, that the boy did not betray the most beautiful one even under the pain of torture (whose tools he envisioned numerous times over the following few days and the headmaster as living proof of the hypothesis that punctuality, discipline and order were indeed only secondary virtues). But that the boy, it just occurs to me now, went so far as to imagine himself in a concentration camp and the headmaster as a henchman of a fascist regime, that he indeed saw himself as a martyr of love is by no means a point of pride whatsoever.

56

Back then anyone who was of a different opinion as to the so-called Double-Track Decision, nuclear armament in general, or even just the planned expressway was automatically a fascist. Yes, you could have defined anyone who was of a different opinion from the young and no-longer-so-young who'd meet at the Protestant Students' Union or who'd occupied a flat behind the railway station as fascist. By implication that would have also included anyone who thought that environmental protection was of less importance, admired Ronald Reagan or contested the right to abortion. Similarly, a lack of solidarity with the liberation movements of the third world—especially with the revolution in Nicaragua —made you a card-carrying fascist or, in the elevated language the boy affected, of fascistic conviction. It was just that the revolution in the land of his favourite writers had posed the boy with a problem of definition: on the one hand, it was anti-imperialist, which is to say, correspondingly anti-fascistic; on the other, with its mass executions and child soldiers it clearly violated the precept of non-violence, which, from his perspective, necessarily belonged to the anti-fascistic stance. That the South American revolutionaries also carried weapons did not, so far as I remember, strike him as a contradiction, or if it did, it was cancelled out by the guerrillas' peaceful-looking Basque caps and the love poems of Ernesto Cardenal, which he discovered in the thin plywood fruit crate. In general, he found the argument that Hitler would not have been defeated by a peace movement as absurd as the moral question posed to conscientious objectors whether they would not take up arms if their girlfriend were about to be raped in the woods. Not only were political views that differed from their own fascistic or certainly suspect but life ideals were as well, the bourgeois family as such, profit-oriented thinking, focusing on a career and Mercedes Benz limousines (whose stars the boy would snap off the hoods of cars at night). Not to mention certain music styles too, German *Schlager* for example. As if there had never been an uprising in 1968 or as if the student revolts had only now come to their town, there were parents—naturally referred to as old—who stood above it all, who had not confronted their involvement with fascism (psychology was most definitely the new religion). His parents, however, who'd immigrated from the land of his favourite writers, certainly could not be carrying any guilt for Hitler, repressing any feelings for Hitler, or be dealing with Hitler inside themselves at all. And to call them old was simply impossible for him. Be that as it may, last but not least, fashion was also political. Especially in their pietistically oriented town where even young people often still left the house with their hair parted to the side and pleated trousers, with buns and knee-length skirts, the greater part of the inhabitants would have been declared fascists simply because of their clothing were it not for the fact that Heinrich Böll and other heroes of the peace movement had blockaded the military base in Mutlangen wearing those very same square trousers and skirts. There could be no excuse for grey, (too) tight suits and wide ties, and whoever stood in the way of his love, his great love, by definition had to be a Nazi. Shaking with anger as he left the headmaster's office, the boy mumbled one of his favourite lines from Hafiz: Do not let yourself be deceived by our bowed backs, the bow could be aimed at your eye.

57

Brought to Mecca by his frustrated father and all his relatives so that Majnun could beg God to cure his lovesickness, at first Majnun cried, then he laughed, shot up and forwards like the head of a coiled snake, banged his fists on the door of the Kaaba and yelled: 'Yes, I have sold my life to love—it is I—and may I never cease being its slave! They tell me I should separate myself from love, for it is the path of recovery, but I gain strength, health, through love alone; and if love is to die, then I shall die along with it. My nature is the pupil of love! My destiny is nothing but love! O heart empty of love! For that reason, I ask you, O Lord, and beg you in the divine nature of your divinity: Allow love to continue to grow within me, let it live, even if I myself vanish! Allow me to drink from this source, and never let my eye lose this light! If I am intoxicated by the wine of love, make me more intoxicated still. They tell me I must quench the longing for Layla in my heart—but I ask you,

Lord, I beg you: Allow my longing for Layla to grow! Take whatever remains of my life and give it to Layla's being! Do not allow me to ever exact a hair from her head, even if my suffering makes me as thin as a hair. She must punish and chasten me whenever she likes. Only her wine shall forever fill my cup, and my name shall never appear without her seal. My life shall be sacrificed for her beauty, my blood shall be spilt freely, though I burn for her painfully, like a candle, not a single day shall be free of this pain! Let me love, O God, love for love's sake, and make this love a hundred times, a thousand times, boundlessly greater than it has been and is!'

58

Naturally the boy thought of his parents and did not want to add any more worries to those they already had when, instead of going back to class, he snuck back to the bicycle racks. He calmed himself down with the fact that the headmaster had called them and that they therefore knew he was OK. By the afternoon—or at the latest that night—he'd be back home and would gladly accept any storms to come in exchange for his love. At that moment, however, it was impossible for him to take part in class as if nothing had happened. So much had happened, so much more than ever before in his life: the night with its darkness and hours of glory; the evening before already, in the bar, in feverish anticipation; that afternoon of previously unknown fear; the black light behind his eyelids there on the riverbank; and now this too, this, what should he call it? Not a threat of torture (though still a threat of violence), this whole rollercoaster of the last twenty-four or, more precisely, calculating since the second long break, twenty-one hours—how could he be expected to solve maths equations? On the way to the train station he bought the most beautiful one a bouquet of red roses and a bottle of Sekt, rolls, cheese and Nutella for the squat. By the time one of the squatters reacted to the flurry of doorbell rings, the boy called up to the window that, because of his political activities, he'd run away from school, couldn't go home to his old ones, was probably being sought by the pigs and had no idea where to go. Four straight-out lies in a row, the desperation in his voice intentional. The most important thing was that they open the door for him and thus the door back to her mattress, which he never should have been allowed to leave that morning. 'Well, come on upstairs then,' the squatter mumbled sleepily.

59

Even thirty years later it's a bit embarrassing for me to admit that the boy had never done the washing up before. At home, his mother did it as a matter of principle, or if she didn't, then his sister took over; never a man. That's how things were not only between them, coming as they did from another country, but also in his classmates' homes too. I don't want to venture an opinion as to whether the strictly patriarchal division of tasks was common throughout all of West Germany or if the particular religious relationship of his town was to blame; maybe it also had something to do with the fact that almost all of those at the *Gymnasium* were middle class. One has to keep this background in mind if you want to understand the great impact that that inversion of the traditional gender roles behind the railway station had. It was a time—or, rather, a milieu—in which men had something criminal about them, one could say fascistic, and were carriers of a kind of original sin for everything, especially wars, and, accordingly, nuclear armament and possibly even world annihilation which, thanks to the so-called Double-Track Decision, was a real threat. There was a bestseller at the time that everyone, and I mean *every* one, had read called *The Death of Prince Charming*, which, to be honest, isn't a whole lot more original than the title of my journal. The author tells the auto-biographical tale of a man who did not reciprocate her love as she would have wished and why it was he not only hurt her (or, as far as I'm concerned, was just an idiot) but also embodied the male chauvinist pig. And then, on the last page, there's a photograph of his doorway or his window, with maybe even his address, and the graffiti: 'Here lives a woman-hater.' That nailed it! Although the boy hadn't had the opportunity to disappoint a woman yet, it spoke to him somehow and he felt bowled over like those friends-of-women who'd squat down to pee even when there wasn't a toilet to soil far and wide. And so, as soon as the squatter went back to bed immedi-ately after saying hello, the boy got to work clearing the dirty silverware lying around on the sides of the sink and on top of the kitchen table. Traditional gender roles in the squat seemed to be so upside down that the women didn't take part in any chores either. Which was in his favour: when the most beau-tiful one came back from school to the—I don't want to say spick and span but at least unusually clean and straightened out—flat, when she saw the kitchen table that had been set for a second breakfast, the candles which, in spite of the hour, were dancing in the bottlenecks, the bouquet of knee-high roses in their plastic pail of a vase . . . when she saw the boy sitting happily with her flatmates who brought the Sekt from the refrigerator the moment she walked through the door . . . she kissed him on the mouth for a long time in front of everyone and then, after breakfast, took him back to her room and didn't let anyone see him again till evening. But what they heard!

60

'Once the passion of love is fulfilled in the act, the lovers breathe blissfully next to each other,' Ibn 'Arabi writes in *Meccan Openings*, 'and one can hear deep sighs. In this way, the breath streams outward and forms in the lover the image of the beloved.' As to that succession of sounds which not only were heard in the kitchen but—oh my!—must've been heard at the station too, he writes that the letter *hamza*, in Arabic representing the glottal stop between two vowels, as well as the *hā*, which stands for a whispered 'h sound', are both consonants whose point of origin lies deep inside of us, namely, in immediate proximity to the heart. 'At the same time, they belong to the first of the so-called gutturals, or to be more precise, chest sounds, for the *hā* and the hamza are the two consonants that a breathing creature forms in the natural state. The deep sighing which comes out of the lover is so closely connected to the heart, it is the place in which the breath is put into motion and from whence it spreads.' As to kissing, he writes: 'When two lovers kiss each other internally, each breathes the saliva of the other into themselves. With kissing or embracing the breath of the one spreads inside the other and what is breathed out goes through each of the lovers equally.' As to the original source of the breath, he writes: 'When the lover takes a form, he or she loves to moan, for in this outflowing of breath runs the track of that lust which has been striven for. This deep breath has escaped the source of divine love and goes straight through all creatures, for this is how the True One reveals himself to them so that they may recognize Him.' Here one must know that Arabic derives the words 'soul' (*nafs*), 'breath' (*nafas*), and even 'deep sigh, moan' (*tanaffus*) from a single root, *nafusa*, and that all of them are inextricably connected in the mind of the speaker as well as the listener. In the same way, *raḥmān* and *raḥam*, 'merciful' and 'womb', belong together as do *dhikr* and *dhakar*, 'remembrance' and 'penis', as well as *kalām* and *kalm*, 'word' and 'pain'. Writing about ecstasy—no, not Ibn 'Arabi but a contemporary— Shahab al-Din Suhrawardi, who died in the jail of Aleppo in 1191, states: 'It consists in that the ego no longer perceives itself as it is too sunk in the perception of the object of its enchantment. Losing consciousness of everything outside of its beloved, even of annihilation, this is redemption and obliteration.'

61

Keeping in mind my plan (that has already been revised enough), which only foresees thirty pages for despair, I should get to the 'self-annihilation and remaining' straight away, for, as its designation of the condition already states, it not only lasts longer but also proves to be so much richer, more upsetting— I'd like to write subversive—than the union itself. It's just that my son turned fifteen today and, after this morning's argument (yes, even on his birthday), I'm asking myself all the more urgently whether in the light of day the love-crazed boy—who, hoping that his parents were already asleep, turned the key in the latch as quietly as possible—was that much of a jerk. Yet again, yesterday my son didn't get in touch the whole day, didn't answer his mobile, didn't answer my messages until I finally heard him open the front door around ten. Running into the hallway to, despite everything, greet him in a friendly way, with more of a groan than a called-out 'Hi!' he disappeared into his room; I trotted after him, I wanted to at least ask him how he was, where he'd been hiding, if he was hungry, and was gruffly interrupted with a 'Close the door behind you so that the heat doesn't escape, I don't know how many times I have to tell you.' 'You saviour, you!' I sneered—even if only in my thoughts so that at least his coming birthday wouldn't be darkened by an altercation—and fought back the urge to tell him that, basically, the door was open, that, basically, the heating had been on when he left, and I looked past the towel that was basically lying on the floor after his only having used it once. Basically, I avoided mentioning anything and refrained from the criticism that he was really only thinking about his own comfort whereas when I was fifteen I'd tried to save the world—you can still see it on YouTube. The rest of the evening went rather poorly. He ate the lunch I'd warmed up for him with both elbows on the table and without once looking up. Even those questions beginning with a 'how' or a 'why' were answered by a simple 'yes' or 'no' before he snatched the newspaper lying two chairs away. I watched him read the sports pages with a feeling of consternation for one or two minutes then got up and disappeared into my study. 'Please put your dish in the dishwasher yourself.' Half an hour later I'd wanted to at least say goodnight, but I could see through his keyhole that he'd already turned off the light and I didn't trust myself to go in. 'Is it a girl?' I wondered and reformulated an idea of what I was like the first time by rereading the first sixty pages of my manuscript. By the time I baked him the chocolate cake he loves so much before going to bed, I was in a much better mood. In the end, I thought, he's my son, the age is tough, his parents are divorced, and his home depends on the day of the week. This morning I woke up a little earlier than usual to make the birthday boy some muesli with exotic fruit and a freshly squeezed juice on the side. 'I'm already too late!' he snarled as he shuffled past me in the hallway and in response to my puzzled question answered that he had an appointment at Starbucks and therefore had to be out of the house a few minutes earlier than usual. 'Why am I only hearing about that now?' I yelled back and referred to the beautifully set table along with the chocolate cake he loves. Then I roared: 'A response would be nice!' as loud as Majnun at the Kaaba. But is this not also a form of foolishness that love calls forth, that at seven in the morning in the hallway one not only gets in an argument over a chocolate cake but throws the cruellest abuse at the top of one's voice and, blind with rage, stares at the other for at least a minute and has to pull oneself together, or I do in any event, so as not to get physical? If someone had only seen me, secretly filmed me, posted the close-up of my face to

YouTube, all the world would have declared me crazy, possessed by evil spirits or, when the camera panned to the chocolate cake, completely ridiculous. Until now, as far as I know, there's never been a tale of great love told from the perspective of the parent, the parents of the boy or the girl, the two who, naturally, no longer appear to be heroes like Layla and Majnun. Maybe in thirty years' time I'll write about the man, the father, who in the light of day loved much more greatly. By that point, of course, his son will himself be a man, that's how God desires a father. This morning, however, my son didn't even touch the presents on his way out the door.

62

The boy had only cracked the door before his father ripped it open and stood towering before him asking where he'd been since yesterday afternoon and, above all, who he'd spent the night with. 'And just look at you!' Nevertheless, his mother, who in the meantime had walked up, asked him how he was and if she should warm up something to eat. She hadn't even put on her bathrobe, she'd stormed straight from her bed to the door, her hair in curlers. As his parents simultaneously talked at him, the boy only noticed how, both in colour and pattern, his father's shiny pyjamas were similar to the Indian-like covers beneath which not even an hour ago he'd been pressed against the most beautiful one in all creation. 'But his leather slippers look a little fascist somehow,' the boy thought, glancing to the ground after a quick glimpse of his father's face, which was seething with rage, downright fuming. Without even looking at them he could grasp how angry they were; he had to have heard their words, couldn't have considered their worry that absurd. And yet, it was as if they were separated by a glass wall. They had absolutely no power over him; the boy knew that for a fact as he stared at the leather slippers. Not even his father, that man who'd turn every screw, open every jar of marmalade, that quick-tempered and tearful man who never grew tired and even on holiday couldn't sit still for a minute; not even him, his proud, strong, restless father had any more power over him. 'What can he really do?' the boy wondered and finally looked his father in the eye, which suddenly seemed to darken. 'What, in the worst-case scenario, can you really do? Take away my allowance? And? Hit me? Go for it! Throw me out of the house? Do it!' Earlier than expected—after only five or ten minutes according to his calculations—he was sent to his room. Neither his exhausted father's threat to keep him locked up for the rest of the week and, if necessary, away from school, nor his mother's tears (she thought he was on drugs) would have got him to spill even a single syllable about the Arcanum. 'Well, you should,' the boy said to himself as, still euphoric from the charm of the Indian-like covers, he threw himself onto his bed. 'He *should* lock me up—there's no way the old man will have bars put on the windows.' No, the boy wouldn't be dying in jail after all.

63

As he made his way to the smoking area during the first of the long breaks, the boy was overwhelmingly concerned with the question that, thirty years later, would, at best, be marginal: Would the most beautiful one acknowledge him not only down on the riverbank or at the bar but also in the schoolyard? For a long time after they broke up he was barely aware of himself and understood nothing; nevertheless, at that moment I think—so early still and as yet imperceptible to the most beautiful one—he was once again dominated by his ego, which can turn even the greatest of loves into a disaster. He should've just kept on as before, animated and thanking the skies, without pressuring her. He should've gone back to the broad shoulders to cast her tender, conspiratorial glances. What would he have lost? Instead, he got it into his head that he wouldn't kiss her, hug her or even hold her hand. He'd simply say hello, stand next to her and speak with such confidence that all the *Abiturienten* would intuit their connection, that one which was worthy of the name of love. If only he'd learnt from the lover Attar who, far from wanting to appear in front of others with his beloved, did not even want to see her himself. 'Why not?' he was asked. 'This beauty is too sublime for someone like me to be allowed to see,' Attar replied. As I said, during that break the most beautiful one hadn't yet recognized the boy's ego. Before he could even say hello, she nodded with her head in the direction of a teacher who was one of the strict ones. 'PSU!' she called to the boy so quietly that he just barely understood the outline, an outline more magical than any Kabbalah: so, that evening he was to meet her at the Protest Students' Union. Exposing the gap between her teeth for a smile, the most beautiful one then turned to the other *Abiturienten*. Junayd of Baghdad, one of the most esteemed mystics of the turn of the tenth century, wanted to even defy God's command so as not to look at him: 'If He commands me to look upon him, I shall reply: I will not look at you! For the eye in love is not divine, but foreign to God.'

64

Was she really so beautiful? Harun al-Rashid had heard about Majnun's love and desired to see the legendary Layla himself. When she was led into the palace, the caliph found her attractive, if not particularly exceptional. He summoned Majnun, and said, 'Layla, the one who has made you lose your mind, is not that beautiful! I want to bring you a hundred women more beautiful than she.' To which Majnun replied, 'Layla's beauty has not a single flaw, but your eyes are faulty. In order to recognize her beauty, two loving eyes are required, just like mine.'

65

That evening, instead of peace-movement support-ers, members of the citizens' initiative to stop the construction of the expressway (who were for the most part identical) gathered in the Protestant Stu-dents' Union, though the so-called citizen's initiative was a bit curious seeing as that, with their decidedly uncombed hair and multicoloured sweaters, the people did not exactly give the impression of being 'upstanding citizens'. And so men demonstrated their rejection of predominant gender roles with their knitting needles and women sexual exploita-tion through the shapelessness of their dungarees. The ecological balance of the globe was maintained by their orthopedically balanced soles, a preference for the natural with naturally dyed wool socks, the hegemony of rational calculation through the con-tinual deference to one's own feelings. Some carried their defiance of the zeitgeist so far that they even defied the seasons by going barefoot. When the boy in his impatience arrived half an hour early, the meeting room was still closed, not a single light was on. He stretched out his legs and, almost lying down, leant on the entrance, daydreaming that the next person to arrive would be the most beautiful one, her heart racing just as quickly in impatience, and with a single kiss the two would promise not to save the world that very evening; when it was time for them to drive to the station, her hands would stroke the stick shift, a classic gesture, and behind the wheel there'd be an emancipated woman. Words wouldn't be necessary, on the contrary: their silence would increase the excitement so that maybe they'd stop at one of the many dark spots in their town, a delivery lane or a car park, then passionately fall over one another just like he'd seen in films and once at Baggersee Lake. 'Every man has conserved an aspect of God and sleeps with Him wherever he may be,' Baha al-Din Walad once said, and no doubt would also have allowed an Opel Ascona to be the setting for love. 'Wherever young women chirp with their young spouses, they quiver beneath God.' I hope it's not the case, but I don't want to exclude the fact that the boy, loafing around in the entrance to the Protestant Students' Union led his finger to or even —no, not that, please not that—inside his fly when someone who did not turn out to be the most beautiful one spoke to him. In front of him was the fat, bearded man his father's age once again holding his piece of paper that had once again become important, residue leftover from three protests ago. 'Sorry!' the boy started and definitively closed, if it was in fact open, his fly. 'Oh, no big deal,' the poseur reassured him, meaning the blockade of the Ministry of Defence.

66

I'd like to return for a moment to the little death (as orgasm is so expressively called). In the sigh of sexual rapture, that's where one must understand Ibn 'Arabi, in that sigh which is at the same time a moan God breathes through the lovers. Comparable in a Christian sense only to the process of the Eucharist, He is physically present in people. But here already the analogy that, prior to Sufism, the Bible had established between infatuation and the religious sense of love ends. Whereas religions make devotion to God vivid through the example of physical union, I am, on the contrary, referring to the religious experience in order to understand a completely worldly love. They are concerned with the creator; I am concerned with the created. As much as I glorify the boy, fallen in love for the first time, his actual sexual perceptions increased the promise but did not grant him release. He was simply unable to switch off his mind (or, if he was, for only a few moments), which attempted to order whatever his speech evaded and even when he came posed him with the question of what he was supposed to do next. When Baha al-Dīn Walad says that you have to learn a lot in life—'until one knows that one knows nothing'—he's referring to physical union, something which, though perhaps more exciting at first than in later years, only in rare, from a statistic perspective maybe even prophetic, cases contains full flavour. As in religious experience, practise, control of the body and repetition is helpful for sexual experience too. The mystics would stress necessary and continual remembrance of God, ritual, the study of books of various fields of knowledge and, in general, experience of the world and personal maturity so that the lover can lose his or herself in events like the Chinese painter in their own painting. Ecstasy is not simply experienced as something incomprehensible but as a consciously induced demolition of one's judgement. Without stopping to think about their actions (which nevertheless are carried out precisely) and reacting in full or, rather, in an unusually sensible manner to every impulse the lover gives his or herself to the beloved, submits to their will—Islam literally means nothing other than 'submission' so that a Muslim as an active participle is the same person who gives themselves to God, 'a people whom he loves and who love Him,' as is written in Surah 5:54, a passage which is among the most widely quoted by the boy's favourite writers. Like a virtuoso in improvisation who gets lost in a musical structure, who submits to its principles of form to the degree that they believe themselves only to be an executor of its dictates, that the music plays itself, in the heights of ecstasy the lover too is only experience. Though they direct the event every tenth of a second themselves, they take nothing seriously to the right or to the left, becoming, so to speak, one with the situation and forgetting themselves to such a degree that they can no longer differentiate between I and You. 'I am the one I love, and the one I love is I,' Mansur al-Hallaj declared before being crucified in Baghdad in 934 CE: 'There is no other I than mine own in all the world.' It is heaven on earth when— feeling the same way—both the other and the beloved want nothing more, and are only desired. But by whom? This is precisely the place where mysticism speaks of God and more contemporary literature of the dissolution of personality ('Peace! Peace!'), while in Freud it is the oceanic feeling or that very same death which, though appearing infinitesimal in the face of the prophetic challenge perhaps, remains very real: die before you die. Despite all glorification, however, the boy was leagues away from that obliteration which—directed towards the physical and, as far as I'm concerned, limited—can be granted to every human being, not just the saints. In any event, for the first time ever he'd sensed and maybe in a tenth of a second between two thoughts even experienced that one can indeed be something other than only I. How often would the most beautiful one allow him entrance to her mattress? Another two, at the most three times, then the boy would already begin to resemble the tiresome animal you put outside, the dog you throw stones at so it'll leave your street. But that was only his perception, she by no means calculated everything as coldly as the boy would accuse her of; and yet, considering the irrationality of getting involved with a boy who was too young for the smoking area alone, she can't at the same time have been in her right senses. She went for a beer with him after the meeting of the expressway protesters but dropped him off at home to sleep; despite all the excitement, she was thinking about school in the morning, her upcoming exams, and even those parents of his of whom he wasn't thinking at all. As reluctant as I am to admit it, though she was his great love, he was not hers. Or had she perhaps loved him in the light of the day, too?

67

And even though it was thanks to a self-invoked sense of indignation more than anything else, the calculated behaviour and ostensible heartlessness he would later accuse her of to somehow rouse himself from desolation (in vain, of course, as none of his reproaches ever decreased his longing) was precisely what he'd praised as maturity and deliberateness when he was in her favour. If it'd been up to him, after the meeting of the expressway protesters he would not only have accompanied her into the squat but also become a squatter himself and attended school for one reason only: to spend the long breaks with her. No kidding: while people were busy discussing the demonstration (which he—'that's a promise!'— would not screw up again) at the Protestant Students' Union, he was even thinking of proposing marriage so long as he, so long as the two of them, were still living in the small town. As he'd already considered marriage, he now thought more concretely about how and, above all, where they might consummate their union quickly and secretly, whether in Las Vegas or somewhere on that continent where *her* favourite writers came from. Couldn't they write Ernesto Cardenal a passionate letter begging him to seal their great love that was being oppressed by reactionary powers? And wouldn't the South American revolution be a life's mission as equally inspiring to the most beautiful one? Later, in the car, he brought it up casually enough so that he could say it was a joke if she laughed at him. She didn't. She did not display any reaction whatsoever other than placing her right hand on his left. That was it. That was what he loved about her, and that was what increased his great love even more: she never put a damper on his enthusiasm, but nevertheless stayed in charge. That's exactly why he could allow himself to be so over-the-top, she kept him in check. In his journal he called her the realist, himself the dreamer, gave her credit for her order, himself chaos, in their love he recognized the union of those two halves that were made for each other and, what's more, embodied the principle of Yin and Yang which he'd heard for the first time not even twenty-four hours earlier in the kitchen of the squat. When she shifted gears at the next intersection, he laid his hand on top of hers.

68

If despair is to take up at least the last third of the story, which my memory has already shortened, only three pages remain for me to finish up on the 'self-annihilation and remaining' once and for all. At the same time, I've only just started with the bliss that, more than simply a time and a place, seemed to transform the entire world for ever. Classes, for example, and school. Which is not to say that the transformation of the world was so comprehensive as to turn the boy into an over-achiever; however, from one day to the next, he began to look upon even the strict teachers more compassionately, those folks who'd have to look into the same bored rows day after day until they retired even though they too had possibly once hoped to live authentically. He vowed to do better to the headmaster who had no choice but to discipline a truant and he'd have preferred hugging his classmate when he asked him again if everything was OK. Strange how the tenderness he felt for the most beautiful one was transferred to the playground, which was no longer the hated asphalt desert between two concrete siloes but, at least during the long breaks, a whorl of people full of voices, movements and colours. For the first time ever he paid attention to the trees whose springtime green symbolized his condition, even found the shrubs behind the smoking area mystical, and stood before the riverbank as if confronted with the source of life. I'd best not bother the reader with the comparisons the boy made between a drop of water and the ocean or a beam of light and its origin; nevertheless, I only vaguely remember them and no doubt would find every one of the images in the works of his favourite writers and telefilms (and novels and blockbusters, etc.). And even if merely according to his own standards, it was a violent (as it was his first) act of union that nature bestowed upon the boy there between the warehouse of a shipping company and the car park of a home improvement store as he waited for the most beautiful one: birdsong driving away all the street noise, little daisies winking more happily than in any mountain meadow and a sun which simultaneously sparkled across the water and filled his chest, stomach and even his teeth with warmth. 'Love whomever you want, you will have loved God,' Fakhruddin Iraqi confirms, 'Turn your face wherever you may, it turns to God though you do not know it. It is not false so much as impossible to love anyone other than Him.'

69

The Sufi and, for all intents and purposes, Old Testament teaching that God can be worshipped in all things was expanded by the great systematizer Abdul Karim Jili at the beginning of the fifteenth century when he wrote that the worship of God was also and, in particular, possible in the worship of other gods as God himself had referred to them by the word God. Jili paraphrased God's words 'there is no other God beside Me' in Surah 20:14: 'The beloved Godhead is nothing other than Me. I am the one who manifests in those images of God, in all spheres, and in all natures and every thing which followers of every religion and denomination worship. All of those gods are nothing but Me.'

70

Beyond the schoolyard the most beautiful one was
not at all shy about appearing with the boy, hugging
him, or kissing him—my goodness, what kisses they
were, never again have I experienced such long, passionate kisses—walking hand in hand through the
streets or going to the supermarket where she'd buy
what she needed to make dinner. As if it were yesterday the three cans of peeled tomatoes appear to me
now, the onions, the garlic and the three differently
coloured peppers in a net; I can still see the little
bottle of oregano on the shelf that with the sincerity
of a top chef she declared so important, and I still
know the brand of Parmesan cheese in the bag and
that there were two packets of minced meat, beef for
his sake, though a mix would've been cheaper. I can
even remember how, having enough in the squat, the
most beautiful one hadn't needed any pasta and we'd
bought four bottles of Frascati instead—no, I'd have
to make up what we paid for it, thirty years later I

know the limits of my memory. I certainly think she wanted to confuse people too—to affront the squares by taking the boy by his arm. 'It occurred to me: I shall gather the hearts of all people around me,' Baha al-Din Walad notes at a certain point, which, however, I must confess is leagues away from a supermarket; and yet, it seems worthy enough to quote (although I suspect myself of taking the boy's love more and more to be an excuse for me to immerse myself in his favourite writers): 'At once this came to mind: they are all gathered together already. And what's more I thought: it will be too crowded for me among them. I shall have to piss and shit, and I am ashamed. I too should like to fuck and the like. The response arrived. Do whatever you like: fart, shit and so on. Those who want to stay with you will stay despite your indecency. Those who desire greener pastures will seek them. For were you to be free from these indecencies, people would make of you a god, and God has no partners.' Though the supermarket patrons hadn't appeared to have calculated the age difference, as openly as the most beautiful one showed herself in the company of the boy near the school or break after break at the riverbank, it was only a matter of days before their classmates would figure it out and the headmaster would deliver their parents the news. And then there were—keeping, once again, the particularly strict Protestantism of their town in mind—the kisses: in the queue at the supermarket, on the sidewalks, in the car and at red lights and at lights that had already turned green. And then the unabashed hands grabbing his bum and her breasts, the giggling and the eruption of full-blown laughter when they silently communicated with each other about the glances of passers-by or the simultaneous raising of their middle fingers to the back window in response to someone beeping—indeed, thirty years later, I realize the most beautiful one must have understood how wild and dangerous their love was. But even today I still claim the minced meat recipe to be my own.

71

I've already addressed his experience of nature: in order to quote from another book a lot of people were reading back then, Aldous Huxley's *The Doors of Perception* (the intellectual level behind the railway station was somewhat higher than back in the schoolyard where people were still talking about Prince Charming and, in any event, certainly higher than 'Dream and Chaos'), the creation there between the warehouse of a shipping company and the car park of a home improvement store revealed itself as 'repeated from beauty to heightened beauty, from deeper to ever-deeper meaning'. But the beauty of nature wasn't his only discovery: the boy also perceived the perfection of human relationships for the first time the moment he stepped through the doors of the occupied house. Everyone spoke with one another in a friendly, even tender way, and almost every remark had a 'probably' or 'right' added so as to turn it into a question, as if declarative statements were repressive, and they all would take the person they were speaking with by the arm in order to secure their absolute sympathy. And though I may only recall hearing two to three diminutives, there were an enormous wealth of suffixes to understate names, addresses and objects. Imperatives didn't seem to exist at all; if someone wanted something from someone else, they'd lead off the request with an 'I find' in order to turn it into a 'one would have to' so that no one would feel pressured (and the lack of the usual admonition to avoid the word 'man' was similarly gracious). In the best of cases, the reader will laugh at the relationships in which the boy almost saw proof of a utopia or believe I've produced a terrible caricature. But when I imagine Jesus' apostles, a society of Samaritans, or those dervishes who won't touch a dish of rice an ant has crawled into until it leaves on its own so as to not pressure it— well, then the saints must have spoken even more gently or given thanks for every handout not only with an embrace but by immediately falling to their feet as well. And there was something else that touched the boy alone: no one underestimated him for his age, no one expected too much from him or asked him to do things he was perhaps truly too young for, a fourth glass of wine, for example, or where he could buy hashish on his own. Conversely, no one stopped him from taking the joint which was making the rounds and acting as if he were inhaling deep into his lungs when he was really only taking a puff. It wasn't apathy, they cared about him, he could tell because of his age, but it was pleasant. Like older brothers and sisters, the squatters made sure there were limits for the boy, though they didn't let him know. When some hits of LSD made the rounds—he'd heard wonders about it for the first time—the fact that he was not included was so natural that it was only in retrospect that he noticed he was the only one who hadn't been asked. Of course, in the end some of that gentleness which impressed him so much just had to do with people being high.

72

The boy discovered *The Doors of Perception* on top of a stack of narrowly printed books while adhering to the unusual (for the squat) imperative of a sign and sitting while having a pee. To learn more about the hallucinations the squatters had declared so wondrous, whenever he attended other calls of nature too he'd pick up the little tome, read a sentence, another time three, so that he began to spend ever-longer periods of time there. Afraid that the most beautiful one might gradually grow worried about his digestion, he finally brought Huxley's book into the kitchen and asked whose it was. 'Yours, as long as you're reading it.' That, or something like it, was the Communard-like answer he received. As I've said, he had his own favourite writers and, without being able to reconstruct the connection he established with religious ecstasy, even today I am embarrassed by how, the next time they were all sitting around in the kitchen, he gave approving nods while with the fervour of a preacher declared tripping (something he had never, mind you, experienced) a form of communion. That he was looking out of the corner of his eye to see if the most beautiful girl in the squat was looking back at him approvingly, maybe even appreciatively, requires no sign. I'm mentioning *The Doors of Perception* in such detail because I got hold of a copy and studied it again for the first time in thirty years. I was curious to see which description the boy's sermon was based on. Naturally, it wasn't the boy but Aldous Huxley who established a connection between his experience and the *visio beatifica*. Not only the experience but the whole meaning the boy had given it, from A to Z, was copied. Had none of the squatters going to answer nature's call ever looked into the books piled up next to the toilet? Apparently not. The intellectual level behind the railway station wasn't any greater than in the schoolyard after all. In any event, no one in the kitchen, not even the most beautiful one (who at the same time was the smartest and most well read), noticed that the boy was simply repeating what he'd discovered on the john. That, or they didn't make him aware of his own limitations.

73

Should the despair which reigned for so much longer, years and decades even—which may even reign today—the devastating despair of their separation, the torture of longing and the chains of wasting away still find any place in my story at all? Must I refrain from describing the lover's day-to-day in order to finish up the 'self-annihilation and remaining' once and for all (already the phrase 'day-to-day' sounds like the result of years and decades of a relationship, I notice, when in reality I'm speaking of not more than a week)? Well, without any ado, today I'd like to reflect upon the time and place that love seemed the greatest to the boy. The demonstration against the expressway that immediately comes to mind is, however, not all that spectacular now and certainly not as exciting as the nights with the most beautiful one have remained. It was a timid march through a, I don't want to say side street, but even for the straightforward relations of their town hardly a trafficked one and one in which there wasn't even a single store. There were so few expressway protesters—who, in the end, were not identical to those in the peace movement or, at best, simply made up its tough core—that the authorities only had to block off one lane. What's even more demoralizing than the drivers giving them the finger from the other one going down in history as having been right is the fact that the fight against the mania for progress more than just fizzled out: it was completely forgotten. You've only got to visit my hometown's website to find the expressway running behind the station praised on the first page. But that's exactly what I want to talk about: that afternoon didn't once seem dramatic, subversive or even apocalyptic to the boy, he who'd blocked a ministry. I'd also like to mention the inconspicuousness of the outer appearances, for therein lies a truth about 'self-annihilation and remaining' which is emphasized in many treatises. Love, if at all, stands in a negative relation to commotion. Similarly, the specific lies in this memory of the day-to-day; indeed, in the very first appearance of duration as of yet untainted by custom. In Shiraz at the end of the twelfth century, Ruzbihan Baqli was not thinking about two youngsters who eight hundred years later in a small West German town would protest against an expressway; and yet, his definition of 'self-annihilation and remaining' as that condition which 'without beginning forever after persists' can be linked to that love which seems to me to be the greatest there where two lovers first have the impression that they've known each other forever and at the same time the idea of ever separating remains inconceivable. 'Intoxication is the playground of children,' Ali al-Hujwiri, who died two hundred years before Baqli in Lahore, pointed out, 'but sobriety is the death-field of men.'

74

I connect the first appearance of duration-as-of-yet-
untainted-by-custom (the protest against the expressway being just one example) to that first smile she
gave him without any particular reason. Side by side
the two lovers walked in the middle of the quiet
crowd of expressway protesters who, thanks to their
miserable numbers, were all the more determined to
defy those drivers giving them the finger from the
other lane. In the boy at least a feeling had formed
that the mania for progress was an even greater
adversary than nuclear armament. That they would
be unable to stop the construction of the expressway
became clear that day at the latest, having been made
obvious by the lack of support for any resistance.
Even without any political expertise the boy could
anticipate that the houses behind the station would
soon be cleared and the same night torn down. And
yet, the most beautiful one and he wouldn't give up,
they'd keep marching together, side by side just like

they had that day: for the environment, for peace and, more preferably, for the South American revolution. While the boy imagined their shared future together with a grim face—that future which would begin the following morning already with civil disobedience and then escalate through hunger strikes and acts of sabotage against the construction site, culminating with expulsion, police custody and, if necessary, even martyrdom in a concentration camp—from out of the corner of his eye he saw that the most beautiful girl of all the expressway protesters was smiling at him, that she'd spread her lips for a satisfied laugh and, as if set free, revealed the beautiful gap between her teeth without his having made fun of her almost closed lips or joked while talking, jokes he'd remembered just for her; without having been in bed next to her or tickling her lightly on the soles of her feet with his toes; but for no reason at all or, rather, simply because she wanted to be where she was: marching side by side for a better world. Woe to the reader who would thus give two lovers the finger.

75

Asked what he would say to a person 'who drank a glass of wine and became intoxicated from eternity to eternity', Bayazid Bastami, the famous ninth-century Sufi saint replied: 'I do not know. But this much I do know, that there is a person who drinks oceans of eternity in a single day and night and then asks for more.'

76

As today my story has reached its final quarter, I must finally begin with that despair which similarly dominated the mystics for such an abnormal length of time. Why else does it take up so many of their verses compared to fulfilment? In Nizami's *Layla and Majnun*, for example (to mention just this one relationship, which relates to the boy's experience so much better), in Nizami's great love there is one chapter of introduction, one for their union, and fifty-two to cover separation, longing and decline. As breezily as the most beautiful one had seemed to smile at him at the demonstration, he could not understand why just a few afternoons later she didn't get in touch, didn't call him back and was not at home when he rang at the door. She never even left a message. And yet, that morning they had spent both breaks wrapped in each other's arms by the river, and it was for that reason only that they hadn't arranged to meet later (appointments sounding far too close to punctuality, discipline and order); furthermore, as it was, they managed to meet every afternoon, or evening at the latest, whether it was to eat an ice cream in front of the station or in their battle against nuclear armament without making any appointments beforehand anyway. Ibn 'Arabi deals exclusively with Majnun's pain in *Meccan Offerings*, never fulfilment, with the exception of that scene in which Layla offers herself to him. Screaming loudly, Majnun longed for her: 'Layla, Layla!' as the clumps of ice he'd laid upon his chest melted more quickly than on a glowing stove. 'I am the one you long for,' Layla said to the foolish boy: 'I am the one you desire; I am your beloved, the refreshment of your being, I am Layla!' Majnun turned towards her and yelled: 'Away from my sight! For the love I feel for you has me so completely in its clutches, that I have no time for you.' Ibn 'Arabi specifically stresses the fulfilment to be recognized in Majnun's answer: 'Just such a condition is the most exquisite and select one can experience in love.' All the same, I think Ibn 'Arabi would've given the boy the finger.

77

Before I move on to their separation, so as to talk about longing and wasting away, I have to return to their union one last time; for there was a moment, a thought even, longer than a tenth of a second, during which the boy with as little as practice, control of his body and repetition had prepared him for the mattress, he more than just neared that obliteration, which—directed towards the physical and, in my opinion, therefore limited—can be granted to every human being, not just the saints. Strictly speaking, he didn't get any closer but moved away again and would only become conscious of their union in retrospect. The fact that contemplation sets in is perhaps itself the direct cause of melancholia, something which Galen already described in the second century. Ibn 'Arabi awards the former's oft-maligned declaration *Post coitum omne animal triste* a deeper meaning when he equivocates post-coital languor with the veil that divides human beings from the truth. The lover must raise themselves above their nature in order to identify the Creator in the beloved. If I understand Ibn 'Arabi correctly, the lover turns melancholic because they recognize that their union with the beloved was only imagined—the illusion resides in the fact that one considers the union to be an illusion to start with. A thought that is as alluring as it is maddening: we dream precisely there where we think we're awake. Thrown back onto themselves, 'the lover finds displeasure in his or her nature and the inseparable bond their soul chains to being. This nature is fundamentally their own, they will never be able to remove themselves.' Thanks to whatever texts he'd been reading, the boy—thirty years later, I know it now from the first and the second and every union thereafter I can clearly remember—sensed that after such so-called fulfilment which had not caused the skies to fall like in the movies or that one evening he'd observed it at Baggersee Lake, a sense of fulfilment that had been bestowed on him in particular, the boy felt that was the time he should caress the most beautiful one again, that he should strive to maintain their connection. However, this contradicted his sentiment longer than just a tenth of a second, and could only be temporarily feigned. As he'd learnt from the most beautiful one, it would've been truly authentic to turn from her and look at the fire-yellow wall or, even better, close his eyes. Instead, his mouth and all ten fingers once again raced up and down her body like a cleaning crew through the hallway that connected the two buildings of the *Gymnasium*. 'Only the real lover will never be gripped by such languor, for they know how things truly are and are not deceived by illusion.'

78

Whether they'd found out from the headmaster or some other person who'd presumed to supervise two lovers, the most beautiful one's parents were now standing in front of the occupied house, unannounced, and asking to be let inside. 'It'd be better for you to stay in my room,' the most beautiful one told the boy as she hurriedly got dressed in order to bring her parents up into the kitchen where the knee-high roses were still in bloom in their plastic pail. At times every one of us makes an absolute mess of our lives, something everyone else recognizes (and, sadly, does not overlook). What's more, when observed from outside, these moments really are disastrous and, though they may not change the path of the world, they can indeed cause an unpleasant turn in one's own destiny; as such, they are, so to speak, acts between humans and humanity. That the boy—instead of listening to the most beautiful one as a lover should—got dressed in order to man up for once in front of her parents and the other squatters belongs to such slipups that make a mockery of reason. I've got to assume he really expected that the sight of a soon-to-be son-in-law who, in spite of the spring-like temperatures, wore three different coloured cotton sweaters over his blue-and-white striped dungarees, had puffed up his long curls into a medicine-ball sized sphere, wore tiny metal-rimmed specs and had fuzz on his cheeks (all of which identified him as a fifteen-year-old, of course) would be somehow reassuring. The fact that his Birkenstocks were brand new did not help dispel the impression of something scruffy, dissolute, indeed immoral, which in their piously minded town had something blasphemous about it. Nonetheless, the boy wasn't that blind: he could see the horror in the eyes of his soon-to-be parents-in-law who lived in one of the villages in the surrounding area where even all the young people still left the house with parted hair and pleated trousers, with braids and knee-length skirts. When I remember them now, I see two insecure, heartrendingly sad, conservative yet good-hearted people pleading rather than demanding to be heard who must have felt more alien and uncomfortable in the kitchen of the squat than the boy ever did in the smoking area. The father almost pitifully narrow-chested in a grey suit, his shoulders bent slightly forward, his white collar buttoned tight even without a tie; the knee-length skirt of the most beautiful one's similarly delicate mother, an earth-coloured blouse with ruffles, her grey-streaked hair bound in the back with a net. When the boy stuck out his hand to greet them, however, and her parents took half a step back, he saw only two intruders, two ignoramuses and enemies of love he'd never allow to pass, not even upon pain of death. They were probably supporters of nuclear weapons and expressways too; in other words, the holders of fascist tendencies.

79

If possible, I must explain the most beautiful one's goodwill not by means of an emancipatory moment but an anecdote which belongs to the most famous of all of Sufi literature: Jesus and his apostles came upon a dead, already half-rotten dog whose mouth is open. 'How terribly he stinks,' the apostles say and turn away disgusted. Jesus, however, says: 'Look how beautifully his white teeth shine!'

80

The reader will think that I mentioned the debacles of meeting with the most beautiful one's parents or, before that, metaphysical languor—which in more recent literature is explained as being hormonal and pathologized as post-coital dysphoria (in serious cases serotonin blockers are shown)—in order to once and for all begin with despair. And it's true, I wanted to bring up reasons why she no longer got in touch, didn't call back, and was not at home when the boy rang at her door. By describing the nights that, despite their bliss, never once caused the empty wine bottles to tip over or his outrageous appearance in the kitchen I hoped to make her retreat as plausible as I could. The truth is that I don't have the faintest idea. Her parents' visit, in any event, did not cause any visible turn in the boy's destiny, for the most beautiful one stood next to him and pointedly took hold of his hand as her mother broke into tears and her father mentioned the pastor as the informer before helplessly mumbling something about the youth welfare office. It can't just have been the boy that outraged the parents so much, but the whole lifestyle behind the station in and of itself, a lifestyle which most likely even exceeded their fears: the dirty silverware long stacked up next to the sink and on the kitchen table again, the empty wine bottles (which only doubled as candle-holders to a small degree) all over the place, the cigarette butts strewn across the floor... and the smell: there was probably still even some hash smoke in the air. And then there were the male squatters with their long hair and beards or some of the women with their butch hair-cuts sprawled throughout the kitchen. 'We're the people our parents warned us about,' was one of the expressions hanging on thousands of doors in West Germany at the time. But there must've been some-thing trustworthy about the boy, and the boy alone, to the lamblike parents. With his impassioned tone of voice and his hands that kept pointing to the ceiling in an imploring fashion, he could've been a preacher. If they were as well versed in the Bible as I imagine and, as Pietists, possibly even understood something of Christian mysticism, then the images that the boy quoted from his favourite authors couldn't have been completely foreign to them: love as bird and nest, feather and wing, air and flight, hunter and hunted, direction of prayer and the one who prays, ruler and subject, sword and sheath, wound and balm, beings and characteristics. Be that as it may, for the most beautiful one's parents the kitchen of the squat (which more than just smelt of hash) didn't seem to be the proper place to discuss the relationship between mystic and profane love across various religions, and they probably did not understand the Song of Songs in as literal a fashion as is common with other biblical passages in Pietistic exegesis. In general, the boy's appearance was less an offer to talk than a declaration of war (the bent backs likewise got their chance to speak again). Thirty years later, I can understand how, as upset as the most beautiful one was by all the excitement, his sermon might have put her off or at least disconcerted her, seeing as that he had his own parents in mind first and only then her own. In any event, she did not say a thing or even roll her eyes. She simply took him back to her room once her parents had left the squat empty-handed and let that night turn into a celebration too. The truth is, in the two lovers I still recognize those famous halves that have been made for each other as well as the principle of the Yin and the Yang, which I have read a lot about since then. However, I don't want to talk about dreams and chaos any more, but bird and nest, feather and wing, beings and characteristics.

81

No, the in total three nights the boy spent with the most beautiful one weren't the fiasco they may have sounded like as of late. Nor were they a continual celebration. The nights were filled in another fashion than he'd seen in movies and observed once at Baggersee Lake. For the most part they were spent discussing things while wrapped up in each other's arms beneath the Indian-like covers (they had so much to tell each other, though I can't remember a single topic) or relaxing together in silence, listening to ten- or fifteen-year-old music—his feet tucked between her legs, her head on his arm—and gently stroking each other with their fingertips, reading their favourite writers out loud to each other, and, from the second night on, falling asleep early enough so that in the morning she could bring him tea and he'd still be on time for school. As for their union . . . well, it neither caused the skies to fall nor the bottles to tip over; all the same, it bestowed a sensation upon the boy in a literal sense that no drug ever could. As far as I'm able to reconstruct it thirty years later —sadly the boy lacked any way of knowing her sensations—she must've enjoyed those nights too otherwise she wouldn't have invited him back to her mattress a second and a third time. Good heavens, why not a fourth time? As a nineteen-year-old, she wouldn't have had all that much more practise, bodily control and experience, especially as the sexual revolution had not thrown life behind the station into complete disarray. The squatters tried to step through the doors of knowledge with the help of drugs, not love, which they practised in a much more traditional way than the most beautiful one's parents feared. In terms of freedom, bringing a fifteen-year-old to the kitchen meetings was almost a step too far for the strict core of the peace movement and thereby the citizens' initiative against the construction of the expressway. At the end of the day, the changing of underwear, naked sunbathing and squatting to pee was tolerated at demonstrations only because, in such circumstances, nudity had absolutely no erotic charge. That sexuality was virtually negated, dismissed as a form of repression one had overcome, does not make the time any more likable; maybe one justifiably remembers it more for its curious fashions, knitting men and shapelessly dressed women.

82

I should like to take this opportunity to clarify something. Or rather, thirty years later, firmly contradict both the boy as well as Aldous Huxley, who declared drug intoxication akin to communion: the temporary dissolution of one's own subjectivity (the 'oceanic feeling')—which I no longer have to imitate, knowing the high well enough from personal experience—fundamentally differs from the experience of God to which the Christian and Islamic mystics testify. The occasion, to mention it straight away, is a book from the year 1957 that I came across because it analyses *The Doors of Perception* in terms of its relevance within the field of religious studies. That's right: this story is turning into a study, I can see that myself and ask the reader's forgiveness now that I am attempting to understand all the more urgently—having said that, it's my story not theirs! In *Mysticism: Sacred and Profane* the renowned British historian of religion and mystic experience R. C. Zaehner points out that the impression of being connected to one's outer environment or, what's more, of merging into it, is not as uncommon as Huxley assumes. In both mania and aesthetic experience one can feel that one has lost one's personality in the seen or heard just like the Chinese painter in their painting. What the mystics, on the contrary, believe—most succinctly expressed, I find, in Iraqi's statement 'The one who loses his or herself in God is not God himself'—is the dissolution of one's own ego in another, all-encompassing subjectivity. 'To state, then, or imply, as Huxley does, that his own experience is either identical with, or comparable to, either the Christian beatific vision or to what the Hindus call 'Being–Self-Awareness–Bliss' is to state or to imply an obvious untruth'. After examining in detail the differences between religious and profane descriptions of the annihilation of ego in terms of linguistics, the mind and the history of ideas, on page 206, Zaehner mentions that physical love certainly offers a reasonable, even functional, similarity to mystical experience. Instead of dissolving in a general, external environment like that of drug intoxication, in sexual ecstasy subjectivity dissolves within a concrete counterpart the lover penetrates but at the same time receives. 'To drive home the close parallel between the sexual act and the mystical union with God may seem blasphemous today. Yet the blasphemy is not in the comparison, but the degrading of the one act in which man is capable that makes him like God in both the intensity in the union with his partner and in the fact that by this union he is a co-creator with God. Thus adultery and fornication are under all circumstances forbidden because they are a desecration of a holy thing. They are a misuse of what is most godlike in man.' Although the sexual revolution had not thrown life behind the station into complete disarray, the squat saw debauchery in a much more relaxed way and adultery was not so much condemned outright as marriage was considered an outdated institution. Great though it may have been, Zaehner would no doubt have denied the boy's love any relevance of a religious nature for other reasons, too.

83

Seeing as that the sex was not as wild as the most beautiful one's parents feared, one can by no means talk of adultery in the love life of a boy who was not even old enough to stand in the smoking area. Reflecting on the meaning of the prohibition even without the sacrament or covenant, however, it becomes clear that it relates to the pain the betrayer or the betrayed will experience; and it is in this sense, that of infidelity and betrayal, that the boy continuously worried the most beautiful one liked someone else more than him. Love was only free in revolutionary theory; in any event, youthful infatuation—which alone is comparable, connatural, not only to the symptoms of the mystic's 'drowning'—regards even the very first kiss to be a promise and more: a covenant, a sacrament which, if violated, will be punished with the fires of hell. It's just that the whole dubiousness of divine justice is hereby revealed in that it's not the deceiver who fries but the deceived.

And I'll even go a step further: here on earth the lover alone experiences what Job did. Job's suffering did not fundamentally consist of impoverishment, loneliness and bodily pain; it consisted of the fact that all of his plagues originated with loved ones. Had he not believed in God, he wouldn't have uttered a single complaint. In retrospect, I gladly imagine the boy to have first been plagued by jealousy when he truly had a reason to worry that someone else had spent the night on the most beautiful one's mattress. If I reflect a moment longer, however, inspired by Zaehner's mention of adultery, I have to admit that, in spite of all idealization, his jealousy was completely unfounded; long before their separation, the longing and wasting away had shown itself to an absurd degree. Whether in the smoking area or at the kitchen sessions he constantly looked for a sign of potential infidelity in all of the most beautiful one's gestures and glances, just like in the beginning he'd watched the other students and then the squatters. And if he didn't notice a thing, he feared perfidious betrayal all the more. What all he came up with whenever he had to wait in the smoking area just a few minutes longer than it usually took her to reach the river from the upper hallway of the older students! And, besides the *Doors of Perception*, when sitting on the toilet in the squat more than once he was bothered by the question of who she turned to while he was away. And I'll even go a step further: it was not only out of the fear that the most beautiful one might worry about his digestion that he finally brought Huxley's book with him into the kitchen—he was seriously concerned about her fidelity. Naturally, such mistrust is not at all reasonable. I see that myself. The question, though, is whether in five thousand years a poet ever described a lover as normal or reasonable. I've already mentioned that Majnun literally means 'crazy', schizophrenic in a pathological sense, but in the tenth century even one of the most famous saints of Islamic literature, Abu Bakr Shibli, a respected lawyer and upper-level civil servant before wasting away out of love for God, was placed in psychiatric homes no less than twenty-two times. Once, the caliph sent one of his best doctors to the madhouse who then forced Shibli to swallow medicine. 'You do not have to worry,' Shibli said to the orderlies holding him down. 'This is not an illness one can cure with drugs.'

84

In general, the boy's jealousy was utterly harmless compared to Shibli's, as Shibli couldn't handle anyone speaking to his beloved or even mentioning his name. The boy would never have gone through the schoolyard brandishing a sword like Shibli did through the streets of Baghdad yelling: 'Whoever speaks her name, shall have their head chopped off!' Shibli was even jealous of the rogues who had received God's condemnation. Once, when he heard someone reciting Surah 23:108—'Remain despised therein and do not speak to Me!'—he cried: 'O! If only I were one of them!' And even this level of near hysteria, next to which the boy's jealousy seems excusable, grew more intense. One time when the saint vacillated between shivering and sweating, groaning and yelling, the apostles asked him why he was suddenly so upset: 'I've been gripped by envy for Satan so that my soul burns in the fire of jealousy,' Shibli stammered. 'I sit there thirsting, and God gives something of himself to another: "You have incurred My condemnation until the Day of Judgement" (Surah 38:78). I cannot handle God condemning another. I would rather be condemned myself. Though a condemnation it may be, does it not come from Him?' The highest level of jealousy, however, consists in being jealous of oneself. When asked what true love was, Shibli answered: 'True love consists of your being too jealous of the Beloved to let someone like yourself love Him.' Well, this doesn't have anything more to do with the boy whose love would have appeared to Shibli as anything but great. I only mention it to illustrate that jealousy doesn't appear first with despair but is already present in the experience of ecstasy. In the end, Shibli would become famous for being one who came closer to God than any other person at the time and is known as God's favourite or God's lover. On his deathbed, he muttered: 'I have become one with my beloved,' before breathing his last breath. This is the only way the boy's jealousy could have produced separation, longing and wasting away; for perhaps (though he never dared put his mistrust into words) the most beautiful one felt pressured, overwhelmed and constricted by that possession love sadly wants to become. So that no one else would speak the name of his beloved, Shibli went through Baghdad and wrote the word 'God' wherever he found space. Suddenly he heard a voice call out: 'How much longer will you hold on to a name? If you are a man, then seek out the named.'

85

Of course, I continue to consider the most plausible explanation for the most beautiful girl in the whole school no longer getting in touch, not calling back and not being at home when the boy rang at her door to be that she felt pressured, overwhelmed and constricted by his all-too-stormy love. If I remember her letter correctly, however, she accused him of the contrary, of not truly loving her, which is to say, not loving her greatly enough: he had crushed the flower, had proven himself unworthy of the treasure and so on. Could the accusations have been more than just copied? All the same, Shibli held one person to be even more jealous than himself: God. In this context the following anecdote which has been passed down from Shibli's teacher Junayd Baghdadi and another saint from Baghdad, Abu al-Hassan al-Nuri, is of interest. Nuri had a beautiful, cheerful son whom he once brought to Junayd. Junayd, foreseeing the child's imminent death, comforted Nuri and said: 'May God compensate you greatly for your pain!' Three days later, Nuri's son died in an accident. When confronted, Junayd said: 'I saw that Nuri loved this boy, and I knew that God is jealous and would soon carry him away.' In general, the most beautiful one's accusations were as harmless as the boy's jealousy if one compares her letter to the punishment dealt out by a princess whose beauty enraptured a Sufi. Informed of his all-too-stormy love, the princess called upon him and said: 'I may indeed be beautiful, but if you only saw my sister! Here she comes!' When the Sufi turned to look, she had him beheaded. For his part, after a short illness the young boy would be back at school, not even two months later pass all of his classes, four years after that complete his *Abitur*, go to university, establish a family, ruin a marriage and continue onwards along the typical paths of modern-day life.

86

But before I once and for all get to despair, I must mention the parents, the boy's parents, I mean, who naturally made an incredible uproar when he failed to come home the second or even the third day. The boy for his part did not reveal his secret, not even under the threat of not being allowed to leave the house—'Yeah, and?'—of throwing his records into the garbage—'Go for it!'—or of sending him to a boarding school—'Don't you dare!'—and by the time they figured it out the most beautiful one had already dropped him off in front of the door once again and his condition was so desperate—crying, feverish, as if absent from the world—that they could only feel pity, compassion and woe. At that point, of course, the stones hadn't yet flown so that he'd leave her street for good. Even if it would be better for my story because it would sharpen the generational conflict that belongs to *Layla and Majnun* as it does to all classical love dramas, I must admit that my parents were not particularly strict, and were trusting too. In the face of all reason they let the boy go, the boy who after the second night promised never to sleep away from home again, and who after the third night came up with some absurd excuse so as not to lose his allowance. I only vaguely remember what he led his parents to believe, something about a bike accident and a deep ditch or a hole in a construction site he'd fallen into (there weren't any mobile phones of course). And when the workers found him the next morning he pedalled off to school immediately so that he wouldn't miss his maths test. Maybe it was German class or that he wanted to let the friendly person who'd rescued him give him a lift; in any event, the reader truly cannot imagine the swindle the boy concocted and from today's perspective the fact that his parents, after a moment's hesitation, believed him or at least acted as if they did is utterly incomprehensible. I mean, of course the boy, the lover, was a fool, it's just that, after his first experience of ecstasy, his foolishness wasn't as obvious, on the contrary: already thinking about spending a fourth night with the most beautiful one, he pulled out all the stops, made full use of his suddenly renewed childlike charm, and appealed quick-wittedly to his parents' care so that they would send him to his room as swiftly as possible to calm down. This too is what distinguishes lovers: for the sake of the beloved they can stop all outward signs of being in love. Once, the aforementioned Shibli came to Nuri and found him so sunk within himself that not a hair on his body moved. 'From whom did you learn to control yourself so well?' Shibli asked. 'From a cat in front of a mouse hole, but she was much quieter than I,' Nuri replied. Were someone who is not a father or mother themselves to have observed the scene in the hall, they wouldn't have declared the boy crazy but the parents who—in such a state of confusion, in their way blind with love—once again gave him permission to go out. On the other hand, the boy really did look as ragged as someone who'd spent the night in a deep ditch or a hole in a construction site.

87

Her letter is on my desk. The envelope is indeed yellow, a pale yellow. Her felt-tip pen, however, wasn't brown but more a kind of black. On the envelope she drew a sailboat out at sea, a low sun, clouds and even a few seagulls. If her letter was a settling of accounts, I don't understand why she made the effort to embellish the envelope with her own postcard. I'm still hesitant to take the letter out, I've been hesitating for weeks, for twenty-six days to be exact, because I'm afraid that it will be just as banal as the boy's journal, no doubt not as pubescent in the sacralization of her own mood—she was likely out of that age—but all the same, if in a different way, laughable and quite likely rather preachy. With her nineteen years she'd already been able to have profound insights into life, which she rubbed under the boy's nose with the melancholic vision of the extensively experienced. At this moment, though, I'm bewildered for other reasons too. I can physically feel my heart is worried, the result of coming across so many other letters on my search for the most beautiful one's final word, letters I took out of their envelopes for the first time in twenty or thirty years. True friendships that, for me, for you, have vanished into thin air; passionate loves who probably no longer even remember my name; sensations of happiness and despair which I only recognize as my own for being there in black on white (or, in my generation, most often on the grey of old recycled paper). The thought that, here and there, all these people, my friends too, I mean, and not just the girls and young women, all more or less my own age, are moving along the typical paths of modern-day life and that there is thus a whole network of people, of peers, spanning the earth to whom, in theory, I should be connected because our friendship or love was once inviolable makes me shiver. That our shared histories, if not dead, would still be intertwined. A few of the girls or young women whose letters I read were nothing less than epiphanies for me—something verifiable from the standpoint of religious studies! But now I read their letters like the testimonies of disappeared religions. For as great as I continue to believe the boy's love to be, just as in religions, it is attenuated by the fact that it was not to remain the only one: I would end up being in love, surely more profoundly, in any event, over a much longer period of time, fight more passionately, lose more and, at least physically speaking, experience more all-encompassing ecstasy than him. I also know the mother of my son from the time when lovers wrote ten, fifteen-page letters weekly— and how much the discovery that my own wife was once in love with me surprised me. How many wars must we have fought, religious wars in a certain sense, for me to have completely lost my memory? It's impossible to associate that tone of hers from fifteen years ago with the voice I now hear two, three times a month on the phone when we talk about custody for our son, which in the meantime has become trouble-free, straightforward even when we talk about his education. When I see the rugged landscape of grey recycled paper stretching out before my eyes across the whole carpet from the land of my favourite writers, seems like I am looking down from heaven on my own life, all the people small but as assiduous as ants. My generation of forty- or fifty-year-olds was probably the last in West Germany (and beyond) to write letters throughout their youth and therefore able to leave something material behind to be found, decades later, in an old chest and spread out across a carpet. In contrast to previous generations, only youth is recorded now, as if grown-ups had no experiences, no friendships, no loves, no feelings of happiness and despair which might lead them to write ten- and fifteen-page letters. But, who knows, maybe it's true.

88

As superficial as the boy's love must seem to every outsider, as brief as it was, as reticently as it was fought for—she simply did not get in touch with him and his attempts to win her back were limited to a single afternoon beneath her window and then keeping an eye out for her in the bars by the time she had long moved to the city—as little as was at stake (as opposed to the family he would one day ruin), as miserable as his sexual ecstasy, in particular, appeared (to say nothing of her own), my dictum still holds: he never again loved more deeply. I don't remember any more what day it was when the two of them, like all days, were eating an ice cream in front of the railway station whose one fountain defied the grey practicality of the surrounding buildings. There were also a couple of trees and two or three metres away adults would play chess with knee-high figures. Without warning, without thinking about it before-hand, the boy bent over the most beautiful one in order to lick off the two colours of ice cream that had covered her upper and lower lips. Although his eyes were closed, he could see, see with his heart, that she liked the way their mouths touched, sweetened as they were by the taste of strawberry and vanilla. Seen from outside, from the chessboards, say, or from the road where, like every afternoon, a line of cars sat in traffic as if they'd come together for a demonstration supporting the construction of an expressway, from every other point on earth there were just two somewhat curiously dressed young people kissing each other on a normal park bench. The only difference between that kiss and a hundred or a thousand others like it exchanged every day even in their strictly Protestant town was, aside from the gap between her teeth, the two colours of ice cream, nothing more. In the strawberry and vanilla, however, the two lovers could taste all the sweetness God had promised his creation. And not only did it feel as if everything around the park bench had been made just so that the two of them would sit there, if what the Sufis say is true—that the universe is bound to lovers, not lovers to the universe—at that moment, it really was the centre of the universe. 'For some time, I circled God's house,' Bayazid Bastami says. 'When I came to God I noticed that the house had encircled me.' As with children who, having lost themselves in a game or hurt themselves, nothing else exists but the game or their pain, the two of them enjoyed every bit of ice cream. But as opposed to children, they were at the same time conscious of what was, they did not forget themselves, but were aware of everything—the chess players, the fountain, the sounds of motors—without having to give it any meaning. The sense in mystic thought, in *all* mystic thought, is that we must eat from the tree of knowledge so that we can fall back into the state of innocence. Pure experience and absolute consciousness do not first come together in the enlightened or in brief moments of profane enlightenment. The first time we fall in love when we're young, we don't become children (still being half-children ourselves) but we can already taste two kinds of knowledge.

89

'God is the lover who through affirmation is annihilated,' I'd like to say once more together with Ibn 'Arabi (and preferably again and again!) though I'm aware of running the risk that the reader will once and for all lose patience with my story which is supposed to be about two adolescents in a small West German town at the beginning of the 1980s. 'The essential reality can only come about thanks to the activities of the servant; it has therefore to do with an annihilation of God. Intellectual argument and intuitive knowledge can succeed in reaching God's being but not that of the servant nor of the creation. Conversely, the act of God's affirmation is at the same time His annihilation in the world of appearances.' It is clear to me that this point is the most difficult to understand for the one who believes in God and does not in fact believe in God. I beg the reader to nevertheless keep it in mind; if necessary, to study it again and again, or to consider it one more time on the hundredth day. For it contains the core of my story as well as yours, whenever and wherever you experienced your greatest love, it's just that in reality God has slightly disappointing names. And only a few know why the discovery is a good thing.

90

In the same way an accountant sorts through income and expenses, memory sorts through union and separation and even more: the accountant that is my memory, despite all experience, allows union and separation to come one after the other as if there could be some kind of business in the world that, after a short period of gain, only continued to pile up losses. No, love is even more ruinous: it mixes so much pain into happiness that no accountant ever enters it into the books as income. I've already mentioned the jealousy, which didn't set in when he actually had a reason to worry that someone else had spent the night in the most beautiful one's bed. Before I begin with the despair, I still have to talk about the unease, the recurring feeling of insecurity that followed every meeting as to whether he was perhaps only imagining her love; the loss of appetite, the dizzy spells, the mental confusion at school, the outbreaks of downright panic. 'All the lover's limbs and organs reveal illness and insomnia,' Ibn 'Arabi knows. 'Whenever he or she speaks, they do so unconsciously. They cannot muster patience or consistency. They are constantly beset by worries, and moments of sadness come ever more often.' Though the boy's journal may not belong to my favourite bits of writing, it is indeed an aid in reconstructing the sequence of events and it is there that I read that, between the second and third nights he spent at the squat, his German teacher instructed a classmate to take the boy to the first-aid room. Though the journal does not reveal any details, I still know that the boy had been unable to put together a coherent response to one of the teacher's questions. I want to speak about a 'dried-out tube' in a moment; but with his chalk-white skin and glassy eyes, he certainly looked like someone 'who was not from this world' and the teacher who came into the first-aid room to look after him immediately asked if the boy had taken any drugs. But he hadn't, I know that for a fact. The squatters had made sure he didn't take any drugs outside of the occasional puff of a supposed joint. I also remember how the boy sat on the green couch of the small, windowless first-aid room—the back-rest slightly raised, his breath unsteady, next to him the boy who sat next to him in class—and waited for the other teacher who was likely trained as a paramedic. I can remember the teacher the boy had known until then only as one of the supervisors at the schoolyard (not one of the strict ones) and that the teacher felt his pulse and laid his hand on the boy's forehead. After examining him, the teacher said he had to get back to class but that the boy should continue lying down for a while and when he felt better go back to class with his classmate; or, if not, to have his classmate go to the school secretary and ask her to call the boy's mother to come and pick him up. Until I read the section in the journal yesterday, I was certain that those symptoms of obvious illness first appeared after the most beautiful one had left him. The teacher didn't consider his condition alarming; he spoke about eating well, a lack or iron, and getting enough sleep. Ibn 'Arabi too explains the weakness that overcomes the lover in concrete terms with 'the lover's forgoing of tasty and appetizing, creamy and succulent dishes which are a delight to the soul and give the body the shine of health and happiness.' That could be; but he also adds a few reasons that no paramedic would ever come up with. 'Lovers have recognized that the digestive juices create vapours that rise to the brain and dull the senses. Then sleep takes over in order to keep the senses from holding up their beloved and carrying on interior conversations with them. In addition, these vapours set loose energies in their bodies that trigger movements and excite the seed whose random pouring forth is frowned upon by the beloved. All of this leads them to avoid food and drink which are not vital. Therefore, those juices which the body secretes will dry out and this causes the shine of health and happiness to disappear, causes the lover's lips to wilt and their tissue to go limp.' The boy and his classmate remained in the first-aid room and were silent for some time. Eventually the classmate asked the boy, who at that point had regained some colour in his face, if he was all right again. 'I don't know,' the boy answered.

91

The afternoon the most beautiful one in all the schoolyard did not get in touch, did not call back and was not at home when the boy rang at her door, seems like yesterday, indeed, like today, like now, as if at this very minute—when I am in fact sitting at a desk in a comfortable study—I were ringing one buzzer after the other and then all four of the nameless buzzers at once. 'But what is reality?' I ask together with Ibn 'Arabi, where does the dream end when a situation I experienced thirty years ago seems so much clearer to me than a present seemingly covered in hoarfrost in which all sound and light seem to have become somehow muted? I could describe every square centimetre of that iron nameplate: its bright spots where the names were removed; the remainders of the paste where names had only been written on a strip of paper or sellotape, or which maybe came from postal notifications; the request in dark blue marker not to ring before 1 p.m., half on the iron, half on the even greyer plaster; the 'Fuck the Army' sticker with the picture of an enraptured turtle coupling with a military helmet. And yet, at the same time, the scene appears like something from out of a lost world, another life; I still know the plot but could no longer describe the boy from inside, when he had which thoughts, how he came to this or that idea, whether he was driven by hope or pure despair. As if I were someone else, standing on the other side of the street, I can only see him from outside: see his rage, see him begin to throw those little stones he'd collected a whole block away from an unsurfaced stretch of earth first against her window then against all the others without anyone ever opening the door to her mattress. How did he even know that everything was over, such a great love gone after just a few days . . . simply because the most beautiful one hadn't been in contact for a few hours? I suppose the silent house caused him to panic, there being no way all of its inhabitants could be gone at the same time. I suppose he feared some kind of plot, all the squatters giggling next to or under a window, the most beautiful one in the middle, as unapproachable as ever for him, and alone . . . but I can only suppose, imagine it all, deduce the sudden overwhelming worry that, based on the circumstances, overcame him, what befell him . . . And what befell that dervish who, seeing a beautiful princess pass by and thinking she'd smiled in a friendly manner, dropped his bread and who, unable to forget that sweet laughter, cried out of love and spent seven years with the dogs in the street where she lived until the servants noticed what shape he was in and wanted to kill him, but who was then called to the princess in secret and warned to disappear as quickly as possible if he cared for his life. At which the dervish asked for only one piece of information: 'If I am now to be killed, why did you smile at me?' 'I didn't smile at you,' the princess replied, 'I laughed at you because you are such a dimwit.' Of course, I've only come up with the story of the dervish as a plausible explanation of the boy's feelings. In truth, I have no idea what was going on inside of him. And that has nothing, or only a little, to do with a lapse in memory. I think that, on that afternoon and the days to come, the boy himself had no real consciousness upon which a memory could have been formed at all. He was on a form of auto-pilot. That is, so long as it was really him and not the other one on the opposite side of the street, in another world, an increasingly pointless life. 'Don't give me back to myself,' Hallaj pleaded and only laughed again when, in Baghdad in 934 CE, he was executed.

92

As continuing to put it off would keep me from truthfully and candidly describing my great love, I must once and for all mention the humiliations, those hardly believable, until today embarrassing and, above all, so painfully useless self-abasements of which the boy—at least here comparable to Ibn 'Arabi's lover—did not leave out one. 'Love will strike you low until you shamelessly lift every veil and expose every one of your secrets. The deep sighs it brings forth find no end and the tears it causes to flow do not dry up.' In waiting for the most beautiful one in front of the school the next day and the day after that and even the third morning without receiving more than a meagre, nodded hello from tightly pressed lips, or not even a nod, just a twitch in that face turned towards the ground, the boy continued to move along the all-too-common paths of heartache, which he would experience quite often over the years to come. More self-conscious, con-fused and weak than ever he held his ground in the smoking area although she had placed the other *Abiturienten* around her so he wouldn't dare to speak to her. But after she continued to have her flatmates lie for her on the phone and every afternoon behind the station a different squatter called down from the window that the most beautiful wasn't there at the moment, for some reason which I can no longer reconstruct—or maybe for no reason—the boy lost control, stood up in the middle of biology class, ran past the stunned teacher at the lectern, in spite of his Birkenstocks took three steps at a time up into the hallway of the upper forms and tore open every door to see if the most beautiful one in the whole school-yard was hiding from him. By now at the latest all those who graduated from an easily recognizable *Gymnasium* in my hometown between 1983 and 1985 and happen to be reading this story must remember that boy who—wide-eyed and most likely crying and with his clothes and haircut not unlike a scare-crow's—burst into her classroom, looked silently around for something in particular, and then stormed back out the door. Or well, not all graduates, for behind I don't know which door but probably not the very last one he finally discovered her in the second of four rows. She seemed so luminous there in front of the window, her head—not only in the boy's imagination—conferred with something like a halo, her profile with the small nose bent slightly upwards at the tip like a ski jump, under her T-shirt her breasts two hills with little towers at their peaks. Her profile? That's right. Her profile, only her profile, and he instantly grasped what was going on. As all the other *Abiturienten* as well as the teacher turned towards the boy in alarm, she continued staring fixedly at her notebook and with her pen—which she held between two thin fingers just like her cigarette back at the river—with her pen continued writing as if the boy were not just three metres away, as if he did not even exist, as if he were only air. He for his part felt like a stone, a mass of rock, heavy and for the moment incapable of any other movement. I don't know what happened next, whether the teacher spoke to him or someone else came up to him, maybe even calmly put a hand on his arm: here the film has another one of its tears. My memory comes back the moment the boy, uttering a single phrase, springs up onto the desk but slips on one of his orthopedically balanced soles and smacks his head against the table. Feeling no other pain than that of separation, he climbed back onto the desk, now barefoot and yelled 'I love you!' so loudly that it had to have been heard all the way downstairs and then added her name (though it was not actually the name of the most beautiful one in the whole school-yard). The reader can imagine how the most beautiful one reacted to this autodidact of a Casanova rushing ahead so clownishly and envision all the rest: her classmates gently getting him down off the desk and, as instructed by the teacher, accompanying him to the first-aid room; the horror in his mother's eyes once she was informed and his never more absurd question as to whether *she* was OK. God, with what terror I recall that spring onto the desk and how uncomfortable the whole thing proved to be for the boy the rest of his time at school. 'His secret became known everywhere and, as he could not conduct himself in a discreet manner, he now stands igno-miniously exposed in the pillory.' Nevertheless, after lunch (which he didn't touch) he climbed through the window and spent the rest of the afternoon on the sidewalk beneath her window.

93

Of Shibli's hopelessness they say that one day he performed his ritual ablution and then, when he arrived at the entrance to the mosque, a voice called out inside of him. 'Abu Bakr! Are you so pure that you would step foot in our house so audaciously?' Hearing the voice, he turned. The voice said: 'Are you turning away from our courtyard? Where do you intend to go?' He screamed. The voice said: 'Do you mean to defame us?' He stood there silently. The voice said: 'Are you acting as if you can handle our visitation?' Then he screamed so loud that all of Baghdad heard it: 'Save me from You!'

94

The boy who just a few days earlier had held the most beautiful one to be the most compassionate of all could not explain the coldness, the cynicism, the callousness with which she continued to write in her notebook while he literally attested his love for her with his blood (admittedly it was only a scratch, but it bled rather perfectly). 'In all divine characteristics there is compassion, just not in love,' Abu Bakr al-Wasiti could have explained, who, surprisingly for one seeking in God in tenth-century Baghdad, was neither executed nor locked up in an asylum but lived a rather quiet life. 'Within it there is absolutely no mercy. God kills and demands a ransom from the dead.' This is a notable thought that the boy certainly would have misunderstood, taking it polytheistically, as if there were many gods and by chance only his own, the goddess of love, was the cruellest among them. Today I can see that it was not cruelty which led her to act as if the boy were not three metres away, as if he did not exist, as if he were only air. In their relationship she'd reached a position where each and every action would've been cruel. For whatever reasons—and he too would soon understand how human beings, from God's perspective, are always at fault for their own mess—she'd chosen to break up with him; it therefore would've been tough for her to hug him as he got down off the desk as her compassion would have only prolonged his suffering, any attention at all nourished hope. If anyone was at fault, it was the boy who out of pure selfishness, thoughtlessness or, who knows, maybe even a desire for revenge had brought the most beautiful girl in the whole school to a place that in the daylight was much more embarrassing, in terms of moral responsibility more delicate and—as he was a minor—potentially even criminal. 'Know that the lover is your enemy, not your friend,' Ahmad Ghazali says, a thought the boy would only begin to understand many years later when he loved more profoundly, in any event, over a much longer period of time, fought more passionately, lost more and, at least physically speaking, experienced more all-encompassing ecstasy: 'And the beloved is also your enemy, not your friend, for friendship is connected to the complete obliteration of both tracks. As long as there is duality and each is concerned with themselves, enmity shall continue unabated. Friendship exists only in unity. Therefore, the lover and the beloved do not become friends; such does not exist. All disputes, all the torture—in the end, come from the fact that there can never be any friendship between them. By God, a strange situation: within it your very existence is threatened.' If she could be accused of anything, then it was not the harshness with which she broke up with him, but the love she reciprocated although she as the older one could have foreseen the fleeting nature of their union with a bit more of a realistic eye and thereby the pain which she would cause the boy. But this accusation too would be unfair, not only as one would no longer be able to give themselves to another, least of all God to his creation—He loves it, and it loves Him—that creation which, by the light of day, lies to itself even more. For, as Ahmad Ghazali explains, 'To love is utterly He-Existence [She-Existence], and being loved is completely You-Existence'—and, he continues, 'You cannot belong to yourself, you can only belong to the beloved. You are the lover: you may never belong to yourself and never be under the command of yourself.' Her realistic eye notwithstanding—when, despite His omniscience, even God is bitterly disappointed by His creatures—it would have been impossible for the most beautiful one to foresee that the boy would turn out to be such a dimwit. Had there been any hope at all, at the latest it was nullified with his vault onto the desk. At least he didn't go and spray-paint her door one evening to alert people that a manhater lived there. Having said that, *The Death of Prince Charming* didn't honestly belong to his list of favourite books either.

95

At one point, one of the squatters came down to talk with the boy who was keeping watch on the door. The most beautiful one wasn't there, she wasn't in the kitchen or in her room, the squatter lied. But the boy lied more convincingly. He said that he'd seen her at the window and announced that he'd be ready to wait as long as necessary—if need be overnight or the whole week—until he was allowed to see her. His desire to throw himself at her feet was by no means meant figuratively (like the squatter thought), but was directly tied to the question of whether the boy should stretch out across the stained carpet immediately or first take the two steps to her mattress in order to belong to her for ever, to forever be under her command. 'You've got to get her out of your head,' the squatter, who'd swung up to sit next to him on the chest-high wall, assured him. 'She doesn't want anything more to do with you. And no, she definitely doesn't want to discuss the break-up.' But the boy gushed about how soft water will break the hard stone and lectured the squatter on how love fundamentally also had a political dimension and precisely where it occurred between two people. Round table discussions in the kitchen might help convene a plenary assembly and one-on-one talks could possibly have an effect on the most beautiful one but, in the end, it had to do with more than just personal feelings, it had to do with the realization of a utopia that could serve as an example. The boy was convinced he sounded totally lucid, that he presented his arguments as sophisticatedly as he had at the Protestant Students' Union. He admitted his mistakes and analysed their misunderstandings, he declared his vaulting onto the desk foolish and with heartfelt openness acknowledged the differences, indeed complete contrasts, between the most beautiful one and himself, not only their ages but also the more serious differences, indeed complete contrasts, between their characters; she—yes, yes, that again too—the realist, he the dreamer; she was order, he was chaos. But that's what made the wonder of their love so much more incredible, their love that would endure all adversity, overcome every obstacle! On top of the squatters from the kitchen the boy would probably have asked the whole peace movement for support; reconciliation seemed to be of such world-historical importance to him. He would have, that is, if the squatter hadn't jumped off the wall with a shout that has chilled me word for word for thirty years: 'Man, are you fucking nuts!' According to the platform announcement in front of the occupied house, which the boy noticed for the first time ever, it was 5.32 p.m. *Please stand clear of the doors.*

96

My son, who's become the first one to read *Love Writ Large*, accuses me of being too hard on the boy, especially in the final pages. Generally speaking, however, my son's simply stopped reading, which, next to the damaged secondary virtues, is another big issue between us. It's as if he's embarrassed to be seen with books and, in all seriousness, calls literature retarded. What's more, even after tough negotiations led to an agreement to read more than ten pages of an already popular novel for pay, he couldn't bring himself to get through it. I can only guess the amount of time, the importance, what kind of direct influence even his favourite books have on him seeing as that films and TV don't interest him either, he just types things into his computer which immediately disappear as soon as, on those rare occasions, I step into his room. I ask myself where he and all the generations to come will get their stereotypes, which, however it is they make their way to them, have been influencing young love for five thousand years. And what's there to take the place of all those telefilms (and novels, blockbusters, etc.) we find trivial for industrially reproducing a fundamental experience when adolescents themselves do not experience what makes it unique at all, or experience it in a totally different way? In the meantime, this morning while eating his muesli my son mumbled that he'd browsed through the manuscript—which, admittedly, I'd deliberately left in the living room—and found the description of the boy a bit exaggerated, but, in the end, spot on. Apart from the Birkenstocks, his clothes were wicked, the dungarees and the three cotton sweaters, the longest on first and the shortest over top, totally hippy. And the Hendrix-hair was *way* cool. 'You know Hendrix?' 'Of course.' Then he added that he had his doubts about whether the boy's flame from the schoolyard was really all that beautiful, the gap between her teeth notwithstanding, but he could imagine her being really neat, she was so careful with the boy, in a way generous, too, and didn't pay attention to what other people thought. 'Did she for real exist?' 'Yes, the flame for real existed,' I missed the opportunity to correct my son's way of expressing himself in the same way I missed the opportunity to warn him not to eat with his mouth full and instead got him involved in such a long conversation that it would be next to impossible for him to reach school on time. 'He's in love!' I think, my heart racing, 'in love!' because I can't otherwise explain the fact that he read *Love Writ Large* all the way through without mentioning payment even once.

97

A dervish asked Majnun how old he was. 'Nine hundred and fifty-five,' he answered. 'What are you saying? Have you gone mad?' the dervish cried. Majnun replied: 'The supreme point of my life, when Layla showed me her face for just one moment, lasted a thousand years and my natural age, calculated as pure loss, is forty-five.'

98

After that he simply left. Again, I can only guess what was going on inside him, but I can still hear the announcement from the platform: 'the next train is scheduled for departure at 6.19 p.m.' Not even an hour had passed since he'd declared reconciliation with the most beautiful one a task of world-historical proportions, jumped off the wall, walked up to the door, pressed all four anonymous buzzers for the who-knows-how-many-eth-time, waited to see if someone would open it for him now, looked up at the window again, turned around, wanted, I think, to jump back up on the wall but nevertheless stepped back onto the sidewalk. Maybe it was hunger and thirst, maybe he could no longer hold off going to the toilet, or maybe he felt a tinge of pity for his parents who would be going out of their minds with worry, or resignation, or maybe he was still under the illusion that with renewed strength or even a bit of food he'd camp out in front of her door again the next morning, but whatever it was, he set off in the direction of the railway station. As he walked down the block to the platforms he looked back a number of times to make sure she wasn't calling him back from her window and only stopped once he'd reached the pedestrian subway. After one, maybe two minutes he went up the stairs and, coming back out into the light in front of the station, walked straight home. My son's right, of course (I told him the ending last night already), about when the break-up, longing and wasting away really began; he's right that of all the dumb things the boy did the worst was not waiting long enough, if need be overnight or the entire week, until he was allowed to see the most beautiful one. Sooner or later she'd have to have come through the door, the next morning, for example, to go to school. 'Just think,' my son said, 'what could've happened if you'd stayed put on the wall.'

99

The letter, the one I'm supposed to reread after thirty years, is still there on the desk in front of me. It's open already. That yellow envelope with its sea and low sun, its clouds and even a few seagulls is right there, there as if it wanted to rub the world spirit under my nose, telling me that, along with the fight against nuclear armament, my great love belongs to another time, a foreign life. That it neither recognizes the reunited Germany nor the Federal post office, the currency that covers the stamps nor the four-digit postal code on the postmark and that no girl goes by the first name which appears alone in the sender's address any more. Its cursive handwriting isn't taught at school any longer either, a fifteen-year-old today probably couldn't even begin to decipher all those regular cupolas that combine to form a colonnade.

100

Someone once asked Bayazid Bastami, the famous ninth-century Sufi, what the most incredible thing about that sea was. Bayazid answered: 'The most incredible thing about the sea, in my opinion, is that anyone resurfaces at all.'

Translator's Notes

The following works and websites were indispensable in the preparation of this translation:

CHITTICK, William C. *Ibn 'Arabi: Heir to the Prophets.* Oxford: Oneworld Publications, 2005.

HUXLEY, Aldous. *The Doors of Perception* and *Heaven and Hell.* New York: Harper and Row, 1990.

KERMANI, Navid. *The Terror of God. Attar, Job and the Metaphysical Revolt* (Wieland Hoban trans.). Cambridge: Polity Press, 2011.

MUHYIDDIN IBN 'ARABI SOCIETY, THE. Available at: http://-www.ibnarabisociety.org/ (last accessed on 1 October 2018).

NIZAMI. *The Story of Layla and Majnun* (Rudolph Gelpke trans.). New Lebanon, NY: Omega Publications, 2011 (reprinted with permission from original English translation ©Bruno Cassier, Ltd. 1966).

QUANTARA. Available at: https://en.qantara.de/ (last accessed on 1 October 2018).

QURANIC ARABIC CORPUS. Available at: http://corpus.-quran.com/translation.jsp/ (last accessed on 1 October 2018).

VAUGHAN-LEE, Llewellyn. 'Love Is Fire and I Am Wood: Laylâ and Majnûn as a Sufi Allegory of Mystical Love', *The Golden Sufi Center* (Summer 2011). Available at: https://bit.ly/2lpTKCR (last accessed on 1 October 2018).

VITALE, Christopher. 'Fana': Sufism's Notion of Self-Annihilation, or How Rumi Can Explain Why Nirvana is Samsara in Mahayana Buddhism', *networkologies* (17 May 2012). Available at: https:-//bit.ly/1DX3y7B (last accessed on 1 October 2018).

ZAEHNER, R. C. *Mysticism*: *Sacred and Profane*. London: Oxford University Press, 1957.

*

The majority of translations regarding Layla and Majnun are based on Rudolph Gelpke's prose translation. Due to a lack of English counterparts, however, most of the other thinkers and mystics have been translated directly from Navid Kermani's German versions. All errors in interpretation are alas my own.

*

Quotes from the Quran are from various translations and were chosen for their sound.